William Elliot Griffis

Charles Carleton Coffin

War correspondent, traveller, author and statesman

William Elliot Griffis

Charles Carleton Coffin
War correspondent, traveller, author and statesman

ISBN/EAN: 9783337210304

Printed in Europe, USA, Canada, Australia, Japan

Cover: Foto ©Raphael Reischuk / pixelio.de

More available books at **www.hansebooks.com**

Charles Carleton Coffin

*War Correspondent, Traveller,
Author, and Statesman*

By

William Elliot Griffis, D. D.

Author of " Matthew Calbraith Perry," " Sir
William Johnson," and " Townsend
Harris, First American
Envoy to Japan."

Boston
Estes and Lauriat
1898

Colonial Press.
Electrotyped and Printed by
C. H. Simonds & Co.
Boston, U. S. A

Dedicated to

The Generation of Young People whom

Carleton

Helped to Educate for American Citizenship.

Preface

AMONG the million or more readers of " Carleton's " books, are some who will enjoy knowing about him as boy and man. Between condensed autobiography and biography, we have here, let us hope, a binocular, which will yield to the eye a stereoscopic picture, having the solidity and relief of ordinary vision.

Two facts may make one preface. Mrs. Coffin requested me, in a letter dated May 10, 1896, to outline the life and work of her late husband. " Because," said she, " you write in a condensed way that would please Mr. Coffin, and because you could see into Mr. Coffin's motives of life."

With such leisure and ability as one in the active pastorate, who preaches steadily to " town and gown " in a university town, could command, I have cut a cameo rather than chiselled a bust or statue. Many good friends, especially Dr. Edmund Carleton and Rev. H. A. Bridgman, have helped me. To them I herewith return warm thanks.

W. E. G.

ITHACA, N. Y., May 24, 1898.

Contents

ooo

Contents

Charles Carleton Coffin

—

INTRODUCTION

CHARLES CARLETON COFFIN had a face that helped one to believe in God. His whole life was an evidence of Christianity. His was a genial, sunny soul that cheered you. He was an originator and an organizer of happiness. He had no ambition to be rich. His investments were in giving others a start and helping them to win success and joy. He was a soldier of the pen and a knight of truth. He began the good warfare in boyhood. He laid down armor and weapons only on the day that he changed his world. His was a long and beautiful life, worth both the living and the telling. He loved both fact and truth so well that one need write only realities about him. He cared little for flattery, so we shall

13

not flatter him. His own works praise him in the gates.

He had blue eyes that often twinkled with fun, for Mr. Coffin loved a joke. He was fond to his last day of wit, and could make quick repartee. None enjoyed American humor more than he. He pitied the person who could not see a joke until it was made into a diagram, with annotations. In spirit, he was a boy even after three score and ten. The young folks "lived in that mild and magnificent eye." Out of it came sympathy, kindness, helpfulness. We have seen those eyes flash with indignation. Scorn of wrong snapped in them. Before hypocrisy or oppression his glances were as mimic lightning.

We loved to hear that voice. If one that is low is "an excellent thing in woman," one that is rich and deep is becoming to a man. Mr. Coffin's tones were sweet to the ear, persuasive, inspiring. His voice moved men, his acts more.

His was a manly form. Broad-footed and full-boned, he stood nearly six feet high. He was alert, dignified, easily accessible, and responsive even to children. With him, acquaintanceship was quickly made, and friendship long preserved. Those who knew Charles Carleton Coffin respected, honored, loved him. His memory, in the perspective of time, is as our remembrance of his native New Hampshire hills, rugged, sublime, tonic in atmosphere, seat of perpetual beauty. So was he, a moral invigorant, the stimulator to noble action, the centre of spiritual charm.

Who was he, and what did he do that he should have his life-story told?

First of all, he was the noblest work of God, an honest man. Nothing higher than this. The New Hampshire country boy rose to one of the high places in the fourth estate. He became editor of one of Boston's leading daily newspapers. On the battle-field he saw the movements of the mightiest armies and navies ever gathered for combat. As a white lily among war correspondents, he was ever trusted. He not only informed, but he kept in cheer all New England during four years of strain. With his pen he made himself a master of English style. He was a poet, a musician, a traveller, a statesman, and, best of all and always, a Christian. He travelled around the globe, and then told the world's story of liberty and of the war that crushed slavery and state sovereignty and consolidated the Union. With his books he has educated a generation of American boys and girls in patriotism. He died without entering into old age, for he was always ready to entertain a new idea. Let us glance at his name and inheritance. He was well named, and ever appreciated his heritage. In his Christian, middle, and family name, is a suggestion. In each lies a story.

"Charles," as we say, is the Norman form of the old Teutonic Carl, meaning strong, valiant, commanding. The Hungarians named a king Carl.

"Carleton" is the ton or town of Carl or Charles.

"Coffin" in old English meant a cask, chest, casket, box of any kind.

The Latin Cophinum was usually a basket. When Wickliffe translated the Gospel, he rendered the verse at Matt. xiv. 20, "They took up of that which remained over of the broken pieces, twelve coffins full."

The name as a family name is still found in England, but all the Coffins in America are descended from Tristram Coffin, who sailed from Plymouth, England, in 1642, and in 1660 settled in Nantucket. The most ancient seat of the name and family of the Coffins in England is Portledge, in the parish of Alwington. To his house, and last earthly home, in Brookline, Mass., built under his own eye, and in which Charles Carleton Coffin died, he gave the name of Alwington.

"Carleton's" grandfather, Peter Coffin, married Rebecca Hazeltine, of Chester, N. H., whose ancestors had come from England to Salem, Mass., in 1637, and settled at Bradford. Carleton has told something of his ancestry and kin in his "History of Boscawen." In his later years, in the eighties of this century, at the repeated and urgent request of his wife, Carleton wrote out, or, rather, jotted down, some notes for the story of the earlier portion of his life. He was to have written a volume — had his wife succeeded, after due perseverance, in overcoming his modesty — entitled "Recollections of Seventy Years." To this, we, also, that is, the biographer and others, often urged him. It was not to be.

Excepting, then, these hastily jotted notes,

Mr. Coffin never indicated, gave directions, or prepared materials for his biography. To the story of his life, as gathered from his own rough notes, intended for after-reference and elaboration, let us at once proceed, without further introduction.

CHAPTER II

THE Coffins of America are descended from Tristram Coffin of England and Nantucket. Charles Carleton Coffin was born of Revolutionary sires. He first saw light in the southwest corner room of a house which stood on Water Street, in Boscawen, N. H., which his grandfather, Captain Peter Coffin, had built in 1766.

This ancestor, "an energetic, plucky, good-natured, genial man," married Rebecca Hazeltine, of Chester, N. H. When the frame of the house was up and the corner room partitioned off, the bride and groom began housekeeping. Her wedding outfit was a feather bed, a frying-pan, a dinner-pot, and some wooden and pewter plates. She was just the kind of a woman to be the mother of patriots and to make the Revolution a success. The couple had been married nine years, when the

news of the marching of the British upon
Lexington reached Boscawen, on the afternoon
of the 20th of April, 1775. Captain Coffin
mounted his horse and rode to Exeter, to take
part in the Provincial Assembly, which gathered the next day. Two years later, he served
in the campaign against Burgoyne. When the
militia was called to march to Bennington, in
July, 1777, one soldier could not go because
he had no shirt. Mrs. Coffin had a web of
tow cloth in the loom. She at once cut out
the woven part, sat up all night, and made the
required garment, so that he could take his
place in the ranks the next morning. One
month after the making of this shirt, the father
of Charles Carleton Coffin was born, July 15.

When the news of Stark's victory at Bennington came, the call was for every able-
bodied man to turn out, in order to defeat
Burgoyne. Every well man went, including
Carleton's two grandfathers, Captain Peter
Coffin, who had been out in June, though
not in Stark's command, and Eliphalet Kilborn. The women and children were left to
gather in the crops. The wheat was ripe for
the sickle, but there was not a man or boy to

cut it. With her baby, one month old, in her arms, Mrs. Peter Coffin mounted the horse, leaving her other children in care of the oldest, who was but seven years old. The heroine made her way six miles through the woods, fording Black Water River to the log cabin of Enoch Little, on Little Hill, in the present town of Webster. Here were several sons, but the two eldest had gone to Bennington. Enoch, Jr., fourteen years old, could be spared to reap the ripened grain, but he was without shoes, coat, or hat, and his trousers of tow cloth were out at the knee.

"Enoch can go and help you, but he has no coat," said Mrs. Little.

" I can make him a coat," said Mrs. Coffin.

The boy sprang on the horse behind the heroic woman, who, between the baby and the boy, rode upon the horse back to the farm. Enoch took the sickle and went to the wheat field, while Mrs. Coffin made him a coat. She had no cloth, but taking a meal-bag, she cut a hole in the bottom for his head, and two other holes for his arms. Then cutting off the legs of a pair of her stockings, she sewed them on for sleeves, thus completing the garment. Going into the wheat field, she laid her baby, the father of Charles Carleton Coffin, in the shade of a tree, and bound up the cut grain into sheaves.

In 1789, when the youngest child of this Revolutionary heroine was four months old, she was left a widow, with five children. Three were daughters, the eldest being sixteen; and two were sons, the elder being twelve. With rigid economy, thrift, and hard work, she reared her family. In working out the road tax she was allowed four pence half penny for every cart-load of stones dumped into miry places on the highway. She helped the boys fill the cart with stones. While the boy who became Carleton's father managed the steers, hauled and dumped the load, she went on with her knitting.

Of such a daughter of the Revolution and of a Revolutionary sire was Carleton's father born. When he grew to manhood he was "tall in stature, kind-hearted, genial, public-spirited, benevolent, ever ready to relieve suffering and to help on every good cause. He was an intense lover of liberty and was always true to his convictions." He fell in love with Hannah, the daughter of Deacon Eliphalet

Kilborn, of Boscawen, and the couple lived in the old house built by his father. There, after other children had been born, Charles Carleton Coffin, her youngest child, entered this world at 9 A. M., July 26, 1823. From this time forward, the mother never had a well day. After ten years of ill health and suffering, she died from too much calomel and from slow starvation, being able to take but little food on account of canker in her mouth and throat. Carleton, her pet, was very much with her during his child-life, so that his recollections of his mother were ever very clear, very tender, and profoundly influential for good.

The first event whose isolation grew defined in the mind of " the baby new to earth and sky," was an incident of 1825, when he was twenty-three months old. His maternal grandfather had shot a hawk, breaking its wing, and bringing it to the house alive. The boy baby standing in the doorway, all the family being in the yard, always remembered looking at what he called "a hen with a crooked bill." Carleton's recollection of the freshet of August, 1826, when the great slide occurred at the White Mountains, causing the death of the

Willey family, was more detailed.   This event has been thrillingly described by Thomas Starr King.   The irrepressible small boy wanted to "go to meeting" on Sunday.   Being told that he could not, he cried himself to sleep.   When he awoke he mounted his "horse," — a broomstick, — and cantered up the road for a half mile. Captured by a lady, he resisted vigorously, while she pointed to the waters running in white streams down the hills through the flooded meadows and telling him he would be drowned.

Meanwhile the hired man at home was poling the well under the sweep and "the old oaken bucket," thinking the little fellow might have leaned over the curb and tumbled in.   Shortly afterwards he came near disappearing altogether from this world by tumbling into the water-trough, being fished out by his sister Mary.

In the old kitchen, a pair of deer's horns fastened into the wall held the long-barrelled musket which his grandfather had carried in the campaign of 1777.   A round beaver hat, bullet, button, and spoon moulds, and home-made pewter spoons and buttons, were among other things which impressed themselves upon the sensitive films of the child's memory.

Following out the usual small boy's instinct of destruction, he once sallied out down to the "karsey" (causeway) to spear frogs with a weapon made by his brother. It was a sharpened nail in the end of a broomstick. Stepping on a log and making a stab at a "pull paddock," he slipped and fell head foremost into the mud and slime. Scrambling out, he hied homeward, and entering the parlor, filled with company, he was greeted with shouts of laughter. Even worse was it to be dubbed by his brother and the hired man a " mud lark."

Carleton's first and greatest teachers were his mother and father. After these, came formal instruction by means of letters and books, classes and schools. Carleton's religious and dogmatic education began with the New England Primer, and progressed with the hymns of that famous Congregationalist, Doctor Watts. When five years old, at the foot of a long line of boys and girls, he toed the mark, — a crack in the kitchen floor, — and recited verses from the Bible. Sunday-school instruction was then in its beginning at Boscawen.   The first hymn he learned was :

"Life is the time to serve the Lord."

After mastering

"In Adam's fall
We sinned all,"

the infantile ganglions got tangled up between the "sleigh" in the carriage-house, and the act of pussy in mauling the poor little mouse, unmentioned, but of importance, in the couplet :

"The cat doth play,
And after slay."

Having heard of and seen the sleigh before learning the synonym for "kill," the little New Hampshire boy was as much bothered as a Chinese child who first hears one sound which has many meanings, and only gradually clears up the mystery as the ideographs are mastered.

From the very first, the boy had an ear sensitive to music.   The playing of Enoch Little, his first school-teacher, and afterwards his brother-in-law, upon the bass viol, was very sweet. Napoleon was never prouder of his victories at Austerlitz than was little Carleton of his first reward of merit. This was a bit of white paper two inches square, bordered with yellow from the paint-box of a beautiful young lady who had written in the middle, " To a good little boy."

The first social event of importance was the marriage of his sister Apphia to Enoch Little, Nov. 29, 1829, when a room-full of cousins, uncles, and aunts gathered together. After a chapter read from the Bible, and a long address by the clergyman, the marital ceremony was performed, followed by a hymn read and sung, and a prayer. Although this healthy small boy, Carleton, had been given a big slice of wedding cake with white frosting on the top, he felt himself injured, and was hotly jealous of his brother Enoch, who had secured a slice with a big red sugar strawberry on the frosting. After eating voraciously, he hid the remainder of his cake in the mortise of a beam beside the back chamber stairs. On visiting it next morning for secret indulgence, he found that the rats had enjoyed the wedding feast, too. Nothing was left. His first

toy watch was to him an event of vast significance, and he slept with it under his pillow.   When also he had donned his first pair
of trousers, he strutted like a turkey cock and
said, " I look just like a grand sir."   Children
in those days often spoke of men advanced in
years as " grand sirs."

The boy was ten years old when President
Andrew Jackson visited Concord.   Everybody
went to see " Old Hickory."   In the yellow-
bottomed chaise, paterfamilias Coffin took his
boy Carleton and his daughter Elvira, the
former having four pence ha'penny to spend.
Federal currency was not plentiful in those
days, and the people still used the old nomen-
clature, of pounds, shillings, and pence, which
was Teutonic even before it was English or
American.   Rejoicing in his orange, his stick
of candy, and his supply of seed cakes, young
Carleton, from the window of the old North
Meeting House, saw the military parade and
the hero of New Orleans.   With thin features
and white hair, Jackson sat superbly on a white
horse, bowing right and left to the multitude.
Martin Van Buren was one of the party.

Another event, long to be remembered by a

child who had never before been out late at night, was when, with a party of boys seven or eight in number, he went a-spearing on Great Pond. In the calm darkness they walked around the pond down the brook to the falls. With a bright jack-light, made of pitch-pine-knots, everything seemed strange and exciting to the boy who was making his first acquaintance of the wilderness world by night. His brother Enoch speared an eel that weighed four pounds, and a pickerel of the same weight. The party did not get home till 2 A. M., but the expedition was a glorious one and long talked over. The only sad feature in this rich experience was in his mother's worrying while her youngest child was away.

This was in April. On the 20th of August, just after sunset, in the calm summer night, little Carleton looked into his mother's eyes for the last time, and saw the heaving breast gradually become still. It was the first great sorrow of his life.

CHAPTER III

CARLETON'S memories of school-days have little perhaps that is uncommon. He remembers the typical struggle between the teacher and the big boy who, despite resistance, was soundly thrashed. Those were the days of physical rather than moral argument, of punishment before judicial inquiry. Once young Carleton had marked his face with a pencil, making the scholars laugh. Called up by the man behind the desk, and asked whether he had done it purposely, the frightened boy, not knowing what to say, answered first yes, and then no. "Don't tell a lie, sir," roared the master, and down came the blows upon the boy's hands, while up came the sense of injustice and the longing for revenge. The boy took his seat with tingling palms and a heart hot with the sense of wrong, but no tears fell.

It was his father's rule that if the children were punished at school, they should have the punishment repeated at home. This was the sentiment of the time and the method of discipline believed to be best for moulding boys and girls into law-abiding citizens. In the evening, tender-hearted and with pain in his soul, but fearing to relax and let down the bars to admit a herd of evils, the father doomed his son to stay at home, ordering as a punishment the reading of the narrative of Ananias and Sapphira.

From that hour throughout his life Carleton hated this particular scripture. He had told no lie, he did not know what he had said, yet he was old enough to feel the injustice of the punishment. It rankled in memory for years. Temporarily he hated the teacher and the Bible, and the episode diminished for awhile his respect for law and order.

The next ten years of Carleton's life may be told in his own words, as follows:

" The year of 1830 may be taken as a general date for a new order of social life. The years prior to that date were the days of homespun. I remember the loom in the garret, the great and small spinning-wheels, the warping bars, quill wheel, reels, swifts, and other rude mechanisms for spinning and weaving. My eldest sister learned to spin and weave. My second sister Mary and sister Elvira both could spin on the large wheel, but did not learn to weave. I myself learned to twist yarn on the large wheel, and was set to winding it into balls.

" The linen and the tow cloths were bleached on the grass in the orchard, and it was my business to keep it sprinkled during the hot days, to take it in at night and on rainy days, to prevent mildew. In those days a girl began to prepare for marriage as soon as she could use a needle, stitching bits of calico together for quilts. She must spin and weave her own sheets and pillow-cases and blankets.

"All of my clothes, up to the age of fourteen, were homespun. My first ' boughten ' jacket was an olive green broadcloth, — a remnant which was bought cheap because it was a remnant. I wore it at an evening party given by my school-mate. We were twenty or more boys and girls, and I was regarded by my mates with jealousy. I was an aristocrat, all because I wore broadcloth.

" It was the period of open fireplaces. Stoves were just being introduced. We could play blind man's buff in the old kitchen with great zest without running over stoves.

" It was the period of brown bread, apple and milk, boiled dinners, pumpkin pies. We had very little cake. Pork and beans and Indian pudding were standard dishes, only the pudding was eaten first. My father had always been accustomed to that order. His second marriage was in 1835, and my stepmother, or rather my sister Mary, who was teaching school in Concord and had learned the new way, brought about the change in the order of serving the food.

" Prior to 1830 there was no stove in the meeting-house, and the introduction of the first stove brought about a deal of trouble. One man objected, the air stifled him. It was therefore voted that on one Sunday in each month there should be no fire.

" It was a bitter experience, — riding two and one-half miles to meeting, sitting through the long service with the mercury at zero. Only we did not know how cold it was, not having a thermometer. My father purchased

one about 1838.   I think there was one earlier
in the town.

"The Sunday noons were spent around
the fireplaces.   The old men smoked their
pipes.

"In 1835, religious meetings were held in
all the school districts, usually in the kitchens
of the farmhouses.   There was a deep religious
interest.   Protracted meetings, held three days
in succession, were frequently attended by all
the ministers of surrounding towns.   I became
impressed with a sense of my condition as a
sinner, and resolved to become a Christian.   I
united with the church the first Sunday in
May, 1835, in my twelfth year.   I knew very
little about the spiritual life, but I have no
doubt that I have been saved from many
temptations by the course then pursued.   The
thought that I was a member of the church
was ever a restraint in temptation."

The anti-slavery agitation reached Boscawen
in 1835, and Carleton's father became an ardent friend of the slaves.   In the Webster
meeting-house the boy attended a gathering
at which a theological student gave an address,
using an illustration in the peroration which

made a lasting impression upon the youthful mind. At a country barn-raising, the frame was partly up, but the strength of the raisers was gone. " It won't go, it won't go," was the cry. An old man who was making pins threw down his axe, and shouted, " It will go," and put his shoulder to a post, and it did go. So would it be with anti-slavery.

The boy Carleton became an ardent abolitionist from this time forth. He read the *Liberator*, *Herald of Freedom*, *Emancipator*, and all the anti-slavery tracts and pamphlets which he could get hold of. In his bedroom, he had hanging on the wall the picture of a negro in chains. The last thing he saw at night, and the first that met his eyes in the morning, was this picture, with the words, " Am I not a man and a brother ? "

With their usual conservatism, the churches generally were hostile to the movement and methods of the anti-slavery agitation. There was an intense prejudice against the blacks. The only negro in town was a servant girl, who used to sit solitary and alone in the colored people's pew in the gallery. When three families of black folks moved into a deserted house in Boscawen, near Beaver Dam Brook, and their children made their appearance in Corser Hill school, a great commotion at once ensued in the town. After the Sunday evening prayer-meeting, which was for " the conversion of the world," it was agreed by the legal voters that " if the niggers persisted in attending school," it should be discontinued. Accordingly the children left the Corser Hill school, and went into what was, " religiously speaking," a heathen district, where, however, the prejudice against black people was not so strong, and there were received into the school.

Thereupon, out of pure devotion to principle, Carleton's father protested against the action of the Corser Hill people, and, to show his sympathy, gave employment to the negroes even when he did not need their services. Society was against the Africans, and they needed help. They were not particularly nice in their ways, nor were they likely to improve while all the world was against them. Mr. Coffin's idea was to improve them.

About this time Whittier's poems, especially those depicting slave life, had a great influence

upon young Carleton.   Learning the poems, he
declaimed them in schools and lyceums.   The
first week in June, which was not only election
time, but also anniversary week in Concord,
with no end of meetings, was mightily enjoyed
by the future war correspondent.   He attended
them, and listened to Garrison, Thompson,
Weld, Stanton, Abby K. Foster, and other
agitators.   The disruption of the anti-slavery
societies, and the violence of the churches,
were matters of great grief to Carleton's father,
who began early to vote for James G. Birney.
He would not vote for Henry Clay.   When
Carleton's uncle, B. T. Kimball, and his three
sons undertook to sustain the anti-slavery agi-
tator, and also interrupter of church services,
in the meeting-house on Corser Hill, on Sunday
afternoon, the obnoxious orator was removed
by force at the order of the justice of the
peace.   In the disciplinary measures inaugurated by the church, Mr. Kimball and his
three sons and daughters were excommuni-
cated.   This proved an unhappy affair, resulting in great bitterness and dissension.

Carleton thus tells his own story of amateur
soldiering :

"Those were the days of military trainings. In September, 1836, came the mustering of the 21st Regiment, New Hampshire militia.   My brother Frederic was captain of the light infantry.   I played first the triangle and then the drum in his company.   I knew all the evolutions laid down in the book.   The boys of Boscawen formed a company and elected me captain.   I was thirteen years old, full of military ardor.   I drilled them in a few evolutions till they could execute them as well as the best soldiers of the adult companies.   We wore white frocks trimmed with red braid and three-cornered pasteboard caps with a bronzed eagle on the front.   Muster was on Corser Hill.   One of the boys could squeak out a tune on the fife.   One boy played the bass drum, and another the small drum.

"We had a great surprise.   The Bellows Falls Band, from Walpole, New Hampshire, was travelling to play at musters, and as none of the adult companies hired them, they offered their services to us free.

"My company paraded in rear of the meeting-house.   My brother, with the light infantry, was the first company at drill.   He had two

fifes and drums. Nearly all the companies
were parading, but the regimental line had
not been formed when we made our appearance. What a commotion! It was a splendid band of about fifteen members, — two
trombones, cornets, bugles, clarionets, fife.
No other company had more than fifes or
clarionets. It was a grand crash which the band
gave. The next moment the people were as-
tonished to see a company of boys marching
proudly upon the green, — up and down, —
changing front, marching by files, in echelon,
by platoons.

"We took our place in line on the field, were
inspected, reviewed, and complimented by Maj.-
Gen. Anthony Colby, afterwards governor of
the State.

"When I gave the salute, the crowd ap-
plauded. It was the great day of all others in
my boyhood. Several of the farmers gave us
a grand dinner. In the afternoon we took
part in the sham fight with our little cannon,
and covered ourselves with glory — against
the big artillery.

"I think that I manifested good common
sense when, at the close of the day, I com-

plimented the soldiers on their behavior, and resigned my commission. I knew that we could never attain equal glory again, and that it was better to resign when at the zenith of fame than to go out as a fading star."

CHAPTER IV

LET us quote again from Mr. Coffin's autobiographical notes :

"In 1836 my father, catching the speculation fever of the period, accompanied by my uncle and brother-in-law, went to Illinois, and left quite an amount of money for the purchase of government land. My father owned several shares in the Concord Bank. The speculative fever pervaded the entire community, — speculation in lands in Maine and in Illinois. The result was a great inflation of prices, — the issuing of a great amount of promises to pay, with a grand collapse which brought ruin and poverty to many households. The year of 1838 was one of great distress. The wheat and corn crop was scant. Flour was worth $16 a barrel. I remember going often to mill with a grist of oats, which was

bolted into flour for want of wheat. The
Concord Bank failed, — the Western lands were
worthless. Wool could not be sold, and the
shearing for that year was taken to the town
of Nelson, in Cheshire County, and manufactured into satinets and cassimeres, on shares.
One of the pieces of cassimere was dyed with
a claret tinge, from which I had my first Sunday suit.

"Up to this period, nearly all my clothing
was manufactured in the family loom and
cleaned at the clothing and fulling mill. In
very early boyhood, my Sunday suit was a
swallow-tailed coat, and hat of the stove-pipe
pattern.

"The year 1840 was one of great political
excitement, — known to history as the Log
Cabin and Hard Cider Campaign. General
Harrison, the Whig candidate, was popularly
supposed to live in a log cabin and drink hard
cider. On June 17th, there was an immense
gathering of Whigs at Concord. It was one
of the greatest days of my life. Six weeks
prior to that date, I thought of nothing but
the coming event. I was seventeen years old,
with a clear and flexible voice, and I quickly

learned the Harrison songs. I went to the convention with my brothers and cousins, in a four-wheeled lumber wagon, drawn by four horses, with a white banner, having the words 'Boscawen Whig Delegation.' We had flags, and the horses' heads labelled 'Harrison and Tyler.' We had a roasted pig, mince pies, cakes, doughnuts and cheese, and a keg of cider. Before reaching Concord we were joined by the log cabin from Franklin, with coon skins, bear traps, etc., dangling from its sides. Boscawen sent nearly every Whig voter to the meeting. I hurrahed and sung, and was wild with excitement. I remember three of the speakers, — George Wilson, of Keene, Horace Greeley, editor of the New York *Tribune*, a young man, and Henry Wilson, also a young man, both of them natives of New Hampshire. Wilson had attended school with my brother at the academy in Concord, in 1837, then having the high-sounding name of Concord Literary Institute. Wilson was a shoemaker, then residing in Natick, Mass., and was known as the 'Natick Cobbler.' The songs have nearly all faded from memory. I recall one line of our description of the prospective departure

of Van Buren's cabinet from the White
House :

    " ' Let each as we go take a fork and a spoon.'

"There was one entitled ' Up Salt River,'
— descriptive of the approaching fate of the
Democratic party.   Another ran :

" ' Oh, what has caused this great commotion the country
       through ?
  It is the ball, a rolling on
  For Tippecanoe and Tyler too.'

" Then came the chorus :

    " ' Van, Van, is a used-up man.'

" In 1839, I had a fancy that I should like
to be a merchant, and was taken to Newbury-
port and placed with a firm of wholesale and
retail grocers.   I was obliged to be up at 4.30,
open the store, care for the horse, curry him,
swallow my breakfast in a hurry, also my dinner and supper, and close the store at nine.
It was only an experiment on my part, and
after five weeks of such life, finding that I was
compelled to do dishonest work, I concluded
that I never would attempt to be a princely
merchant, and took the stage for home.   It
was a delightful ride home on the top of the

rocking coach, with the driver lashing his whip and his horses doing their best.

" I think it was in 1841 that Daniel Webster attended the Merrimac County Agricultural Fair at Fisherville, now Penacook. I was there with a fine yoke of oxen which won his admiration. He asked me as to their age and weight, and to whom they belonged. He recognized nearly all of his old acquaintances. I saw him many times during the following year. He was in the prime of life, — in personal appearance a remarkable man."

Thus far it will be seen that there was little in Mr. Coffin's life and surroundings that could not be easily told of the average New England youth. Besides summer work on the farm, and " chores " about the house, he had taken several terms at the academy in Boscawen. During the winter of 1841–42, while unable to do any outdoor work, on account of sickness, he bought a text-book on land-surveying and learned something of the science and art, yet more for pastime than from any expectation of making it useful.

Nevertheless, that book had a powerful influence upon his life. It gave him an idea, through the application of measurement to the earth's surface, of that order and beauty of those mathematical principles after which the Creator built the universe. It opened his eyes to the vast modification of the landscape, and the earth itself, by man's work upon its crust. It gave him the engineer's eye. Henceforth he became interested in the capacity of every portion of the country, which came under his notice, for the roads, fields, gardens, and parks of peace, and for the making of forts, military roads, and the strategy of battle. In a word, the book and its study gave him an enrichment of life which fitted him to enjoy the world by travel, and to understand the arena of war, — theatres of usefulness to which Providence was to call him in after-life.

In August, 1843, in his twenty-first year, he became a student at Pembroke Academy. The term of ten weeks seemed ever afterwards in his memory one of the golden periods of his life. The teacher, Charles G. M. Burnham, was enthusiastic and magnetic, having few rules, and placing his pupils upon their honor. It was not so much what Carleton learned from books, as association with the one hundred and sixty young men and women of his own age, which here so stimulated him.

From the academy he advanced to be teacher of the district school on Corser Hill, in West Boscawen, but after three weeks of pedagogy was obliged to leave on account of sickness. He passed the remainder of the winter in lumbering, rising at 4 A. M. to feed his team of horses. While breakfast was preparing he studied books, ate the meal by candle-light, and then was off with his lunch of cold meat, bread, and apple pie. From the woods to the bank of the Merrimac the distance was three miles, and three or four trips were made daily in drawing the long and heavy logs to the water. Returning home after dark, he ate supper by candle-light, fed his horses, and gave an hour to study before bedtime.

The summer of 1844 was one of hard toil on the farm. In July he became of age, and during the autumn worked on his brother-in-law's farm, rising at five and frequently finishing about 9 P. M. It is no wonder that all through his life Mr. Coffin showed a deep sympathy, born of personal experience, with men who are bound down to physical toil.

Nevertheless, the fine arts were not neglected. He had already learned to play the "seraphine," the instrument which has been developed into the reed organ. He started the project, in 1842, of getting one for the church. By great efforts sixty dollars were raised and an instrument purchased in Concord. Mr. Coffin became the "organist," and also taught singing in the schoolhouse. Three of his nieces, excellent singers, assisted him.

The time had now come for the young man to strike out in the world for himself. Like most New England youth, his eyes were on Boston. With a recommendation from his friend, the minister, he took the stage to Concord. The next day he was in Boston, then a city of 75,000 people, with the water dashing against the embankment of Charles Street, opposite the Common, and with only one road leading out to Roxbury. Sloops and schooners, loaded with coal and timber, sailed over the spot where afterwards stood his house, at No. 81 Dartmouth Street. In a word, the "Back Bay" and "South End" were then unknown. Boston city, shaped like a pond lily laid flat, had its long stem reaching to the solid land southward on the Dorchester and Roxbury hills.

Young Carleton went to Mount Vernon Church on Ashburton Place, the pastor, Dr. E. N. Kirk, being in the prime of his power, and the church crowded. The country boy from New Hampshire became a member of the choir and enjoyed the Friday night rehearsals. He found employment at one dollar a day in a commission store, 84 Utica Street, with the firm of Lowell & Hinckley. The former, a brother of James Russell Lowell, had a son, a bright little boy, who afterwards became the superb cavalry commander at the battle of Cedar Creek in 1864. Carleton boarded on Beacon Street, next door to the present Athenæum Building. The firm dissolved by Mr. Lowell's entering the Athenæum. Carleton returned to his native town to vote. He became a farm laborer with his brother-in-law, passing a summer of laborious toil, frequently fourteen and sixteen hours, with but little rest.

It was time now for the old Granite State to be opened by the railway. The Northern Railroad had been chartered, and preliminary

surveys were to be made. Young Carleton,
seizing the opportunity, went to Franklin, saw
the president, and told him who he was. He
was at once offered a position as chainman, and
told to report two weeks later. The other
chainman gave Carleton the leading end, intending that the Boscawen boy, and not himself, should drag it and drive the stake.
Carleton did not object, for he was looking
beyond the chain.

The compass-man was an old gentleman
dim of eyesight and slow of action. Young
Carleton drove his first stake, at a point one
hundred feet north of the Concord railway
depot, which was opened in the month of
August, 1845. The old compass-man then
set his compass for a second sight, but before
he could get out his spectacles and put them
on, young Carleton read the point to him.
When, through his glasses, the old gentleman
had verified the reading, he was delighted.
Promotion for Carleton was now sure. Before
night he was not only dragging the chain, but
was sighting the instrument. The result, two
days later, was promotion to the charge of the
party. What he had learned of land survey-

ing was producing its fruit. In the autumn he was employed as the head of a party to make the preliminary survey of the Concord and Portsmouth road.

Unfortunately, during this surveying campaign, he received a wound which caused slight permanent lameness and disqualified him for military service. It came about in this way. He was engaged in some work while an axe-man behind him was chopping away some bushes and undergrowth. The latter gave a swing of the axe which came out too far and cut through the boot and large tendon of Carleton's left ankle. With skilled medical attention, rest, and care, the wound would have soon healed up, but owing to lack of skill, and to carelessness and exposure, the wound gave him considerable trouble, and once re-opened. In after-life, when overwearied, this part of the limb was very troublesome.

It was not all toil for Carleton. The time of love had already come, and the days of marriage were not far off. The object of his devotion was Miss Sally Russell Farmer, the daughter of Colonel John Farmer, of Boscawen. On February 18, 1846, amid the winter winds, the fire of a holy union for life was kindled, and its glow was unflickering during more than fifty years. In ancestry and relationship, the Farmers of Boscawen were allied with the Russells of England, — Sir William, of bygone centuries, and Lord John, of our own memory. Carleton found a true "help-meet" in Sally Coffin. Though no children ever came to bless their union, it was as perfect, though even more hallowed and beautified, on the day it was severed, as when first begun.

The following summer was one full of days of toil in the engineering department of the Northern railway, Carleton being engaged upon the first section to be opened from Concord to Franklin. The engineering was difficult, and the work heavy. Breakfast was eaten at six in the morning, and dinner wherever it could be found along the road. Seldom could the young engineer rise from his arithmetical calculations until midnight.

Weary with such exacting mental and physical labor, he resigned his position, and became a contractor. First he supplied the Concord

railroad with 200,000 feet of lumber, which
he purchased at the various mills. This ven-
ture being profitable, he engaged in the lumber
trade, furnishing beams for a large factory,
timber for a new railway station at Concord,
and for a ship at Medford. It was while
transacting some business in Lowell, that he
saw President Polk, James Buchanan, Levi
Woodbury, and other political magnates of
the period, who, however, were rather coldly
received on account of the annexation of
Texas, and war with Mexico.

Wishing for a home of his own, Carleton
now bought a farm in West Boscawen, and
began housekeeping in the following November. He carried on extensive lumber operations, hiring a large number of men and teams.
He rose between four and five in the morning,
and was in the woods, four miles away, at
sunrise, working through the day, and reaching home after dark to care for the cattle and
horses and milk the cows. None of his men
worked harder than he.

Although railroad building stimulated prices
and gave activity to business men, the flush
times were followed by depression. To secure

the construction of a railway to the mast yard, Carleton subscribed to the stock, and, under the individual liability law of that period, was compelled to take as much more to relieve the company from debt. Soon he found, however, in spite of hard work for both himself and his wife, that farming and lumbering together rendered no adequate returns. Relief to mind and body was found in the weekly arrival of *Littell's Living Age* and two or three weekly papers, in agricultural meetings at Concord and Manchester, and in the formation of the State Agricultural Society, of which Carleton was one of the founders.

CHAPTER V

THE modern age of electricity was ushered in during Mr. Coffin's early manhood. The telegraph, which has given the world a new nervous system, being less an invention than an evolution, had from the labors of Prof. Joseph Henry, in Albany, and of Wheatstone, of England, become, by Morse's invention of the dot-and-line alphabet, a far-off writer by which men could annihilate time and distance. One of the first to experiment with the new power — old as eternity, but only slowly revealed to man — was Carleton's brother-in-law, Prof. Moses G. Farmer, whose services to science have never yet been adequately set forth.

This inventor in 1851 invited Mr. Coffin to leave the farm temporarily, to construct a line of wire connecting the telegraphs of Boston with the Cambridge observatory, for the purpose of giving uniform time to the railroads.

In this Carleton was so successful that, in the winter and spring of 1852, he was employed by Mr. Moses Farmer to construct the telegraph fire alarm, which had been invented by his brother-in-law. The work was completed in the month of May, and Charles Carleton Coffin gave the first alarm of fire ever transmitted by the electric apparatus. The system was a great curiosity, and many distinguished men of this country, and from Europe, especially from Russia and France, came to inspect its working.

Commodore Charles Wilkes, of the United States Navy, who had returned from his brilliant expedition in Antarctic regions, but who had not yet made himself notorious by a capture of the Confederate commissioners, proposed to use this electric system in ascertaining the velocity of sound. Cannon were stationed at various points, the Navy Yard, Fort Constitution, South Boston, and at the Observatory, in front of which was an apparatus and telegraph connecting with the central office. Each cannon, when fired, heated the circuit. Each listener at the various points was to snap a circuit key the moment the sound reached him. In the central office was a chronograph which registered each discharge in succession. The distances from each cannon muzzle had been obtained by triangulation. In the calm, still night, Commodore Wilkes and Professor Farmer stood in the cupola of the State House with the chronograph, holding their watches, and noting the successive flashes.

The experiments were not very satisfactory. Mr. Coffin, perhaps, possibly, because he was not a skilled artillerist, had the mortifying experience of seeing the apparatus in front of his cannon blown into fragments, but he made notes of the other reports. After a series of trials, the approximate result was obtained, that in a moderately humid atmosphere the velocity of sound was a little under nine hundred feet per second.

The exactions of the fire alarm service, owing to its crude construction, which compelled the attendants to be ever on the alert, told severely on Carleton's nervous system. He therefore resigned in October, and went to Cincinnati to get the system introduced there. Herds of hogs then roamed the streets, picking up their living around the grain houses, and in the gutters. After three weeks of exhibition and canvassing, he found that Cincinnati was not yet ready for such a novelty, and so he returned to Boston.

The following winter was passed in Boscawen without financially remunerative employment, but in earnest study, though in the spring a supply of money came pleasantly and unexpectedly. He undertook to negotiate a patent for an invention of Professor Farmer's, and after considerable time disposed of it to a New York gentleman. Carleton's net profits were $1,850.

This was an immense sum to him, and he once more resolved to try Boston, and did so. He made his home, however, in Malden, renting half of a small house on Washington Street. Having inked his pen on agricultural subjects, descriptive pieces, and even on a few poems, he took up newspaper work. Entering the office of the Boston *Journal*, he worked without pay, giving the *Journal* three months' service in writing editorials, and reporting meetings. This was simply to educate himself as a journalist. At that time very few reporters were employed on the daily papers.

What he says of this work had better be told
in his own words :

"It was three months of hard study and
work. I saw that what the public wanted was
news in condensed form; that the day for stately
editorials was passing away; that short statements and arguments, which went like an ar-
row straight to the mark, were what the public
would be likely to read. I formed my style
of writing with that in view. I avoided long
sentences. I thought that I went too far in
the other direction and clipped my sentences
too short, and did not give sufficient ornamen-
tation, but I determined to use words of Saxon
rather than of Latin or Norman origin, to use
'begin,' instead of 'commence,' as stronger and
more forcible.

"I selected the speeches of Webster, Lord
Erskine, Burke, and other English writers, for
careful analysis, but soon discarded Brougham
and Burke. I derived great benefit from
Erskine and Webster, for incisive and strong
statement, — also Shakespeare and Milton.
At that time I read again and again the
rhapsodies of Christopher North, Professor
Wilson, and the 'Noctes Ambrosianæ,' and

found great delight, also, in reading Bryant's poems.

" It was the period of white heat in the anti-slavery struggle, when the public heard the keenest debates, the sharpest invective. At an anti-slavery meeting the red-hot lava was always on the flow. The anti-slavery men were like anthracite in the furnace, — red hot, — white hot, — clear through. I have little doubt that the sharpness and ruggedness of my writing is due, in some degree, to the curt, sharp statements of that period. When men were feeling so intensely, and speaking with a force and earnestness unknown in these later years, a reporter would insensibly take on something of the spirit of the hour, otherwise his reports would be limp and lifeless. I was induced to study stenography, but the system then in use was complex and inadequate, — hard to learn. I was informed by several stenographers that if I wanted a condensed report it would be far better to give the spirit, rather than attempt the letter."

During the summer of 1854, Mrs. Coffin being in poor health, they visited Saratoga together, passed several weeks at the Springs, and visited the battle-field where his grandfather, Eliphalet Kilborn, had fought. Carleton picked up a bullet just uncovered by the plow, and in that bright and beautiful summer's day the whole scene of 1777 came back before him. From the author's map in " Burgoyne's Defence," giving a meagre sketch of the battle, he was able to retrace the general lines of the American breastworks. This was the first of scores of careful study on the spot and reproduction in imagination of famous battles, which Carleton made and enjoyed during his life.

He was also present at the International Exhibition in New York, seeing, on the opening day, President Franklin Pierce and his Cabinet. The popular idol of the hour was General Winfield Scott, of an imposing personal appearance which was set off by a showy uniform. He was the hero of the two wars, and expected to be President. In personal vanity, in bravery, and in military science, Scott was without a superior, one of the ablest officers whose names adorn the long and brilliant roll of the United States regular army.

Carleton wrote of General Scott: " A man of great egotism, an able general, but who never had any chance of an election. He was the last candidate of a dying political party which never was aggressive and which was going down under the slave power, to which it had allied itself."

Mr. Coffin writes further: "The passage of the Compromise Measures of 1850 gave great offence to the radical wing of the anti-slavery party. The members of that wing were very bitter towards Daniel Webster for his part in its passage. I was heart and soul in sympathy with the grand idea of anti-slavery, but did not believe in fierce denunciation as the best argument. I did not like the compromise, and hated the odious fugitive slave law, but I nevertheless believed that Mr. Webster was sincere in his desire to avert impending trouble. I learned from Hon. G. W. Nesmith, of Franklin, president of the Northern railroad, that Mr. Webster felt very keenly the assaults upon him, and the manifest alienation of his old friends. Mr. Nesmith suggested that his old-time neighbors in Boscawen and Salisbury should send him a letter expressive of their appreciation of his efforts to harmonize the country, and that the proper person to write the letter was the Rev. Mr. Price, ex-pastor of the Congregational church in West Boscawen, in whom the county had great confidence. A few days later, at the invitation of Mr. Price, I went over the rough draft with him in his study. The letter was circulated for signatures by Worcester Webster, of Boscawen, distantly related to Daniel. It is in the published works of the great statesman, edited by Mr. Everett, together with his reply."

In May, 1854, Carleton saw the Potomac and the Capitol at Washington for the first time. The enlargement of the house of the National Legislature had not yet begun. He studied the paintings in the rotunda, which were to him a revelation of artistic power. He spent a long time before Prof. Robert W. Weir's picture of the departure of the Pilgrims for Delfshaven.

Here are some of his impressions of the overgrown village and of the characters he met:

"Washington was a straggling city, thoroughly Southern. There was not a decent hotel. The National was regarded as the best. Nearly all the public men were in boarding-houses. I stopped at the Kirkwood, then regarded as very good. The furniture was old; there was scarcely a whole chair in the parlor or dining-room. It was the period of the Kansas struggle. The passions of men were at a white heat. The typical Southern man wore a broad-brimmed felt hat. Many had long hair and loose flowing neckties. There was insolence and swagger in their deportment towards Northern men.

"I spent much time in the gallery of the Senate. Thomas Benton, of Missouri, was perhaps the most notable man in the Senate. Slidell, of Louisiana, whom I had seen in New Hampshire the winter before, speaking for the Democracy, and Toombs, of Georgia, were strongly marked characters. Toombs made a speech doubling up his fists as if about to knock some one down."

From Washington, Carleton went to Harrisburg, noticing, as he passed over the railway, the difference between free and slave territory. "A half dozen miles from the boundary between Maryland and Pennsylvania was sufficient to change the characteristics of the country." The Pennsylvania railway had just been opened, and Altoona was just starting. Carleton visited the iron and other industries at Pittsburg, and described his journey and impressions in a series of letters to the Boston *Journal*. Having inherited from his father eighty acres of land in Central Illinois, near the town of Lincoln, he went out to visit it. At Chicago, a bustling place of 25,000 inhabitants, he found the mud knee-deep. Great crowds of emigrants were arriving and departing. Going south to La Salle he took steamer on the Illinois River to Peoria, reaching there Saturday night. Not willing to travel on Sunday, he went ashore. After attending service at church, he asked the privilege of playing on the organ. A few minutes later, he found a large audience listening with apparent pleasure.

CHAPTER VI

THE REPUBLICAN PARTY AND ABRAHAM LINCOLN

THE time had now come for the formation of a new political party, and in this
Carleton had a hand, being at the first meeting
and making the acquaintance of the leading
men, Henry Wilson, Anson Burlingame,
George S. Boutwell, N. P. Banks, Charles
Sumner, and others. His connection with the
press brought him into personal contact with
men of all parties. He found Edward Everett more sensitive to criticism than any other
public man.

In 1856 Carleton was offered a position on
the *Atlas*, which had been the leading Whig
paper in Massachusetts. He attended the
first great Republican gathering ever held in
Maine, at Portland, at which Hannibal Hamlin, Benjamin Wade, and N. P. Banks were
speakers. On the night of the Maine election, which was held in August, as the returns,

which gave the first great victory of the Republican party in the Fremont campaign, thrilled the young editor, he wrote a head-line which was copied all over the country,—" Behold How Brightly Breaks the Morning."

In Malden, where he was then residing, a Fremont Club was formed. Carleton wrote a song, to the melody " Suoni La Tromba," from one of the operas then much admired, which was sung by the glee men in the club. Political enthusiasm rose to fever heat. In the columns of the *Atlas* are many editorials which came seething hot from Carleton's brain, during the campaign which elevated Mr. James Buchanan to the presidency.

When the storm of politics had subsided, Carleton wrote a series of articles for an educational periodical, *The Student and Schoolmate.* Inspired by his attendance on the meetings of the American Association for the Advancement of Science, he penned a series of astronomical articles for *The Congregationalist.* He also attended the opening of the Grand Trunk railroad from Montreal to Toronto, celebrated by a grand jubilee at Montreal. During the winter, when Elihu Burritt, the learned blacksmith, failed to appear on the lecture platform, Carleton was called upon at short notice to give his lecture entitled " The Savage and the Citizen."

He was welcomed with applause, which he half suspected was in derision. At the end, he received ten dollars and a vote of thanks. The lecture system was then just beginning, and its bright stars, Phillips, Holmes, Whipple, Beecher, Gough, and Curtis were then mounting the zenith.

Carleton made another trip West in 1857, seeing the Mississippi, when the railway was completed from Cincinnati to St. Louis. When the crowd was near degenerating into a drunken mob, — the native wine of Missouri being served free to everybody, — the committee in charge cut off the supply of drink, and thus saved a riot. From St. Louis he went to Liverpool, on the Illinois River, to see about his land affairs. He enjoyed hugely the strange frontier scenes, meals in log cabins, and the trial of a case in court, which was in a schoolroom lighted by two tallow candles.

The Boston *Atlas*, unable to hold up the world, had summoned the *Bee* to its aid, yet did not even then stand on a paying basis. Finally it became absorbed in the Boston *Traveller*. Carleton again entered the service of the Boston *Journal* as reporter. Yet life was a hard struggle. Through the years 1857, 1858, 1859, Carleton was floating around among the newspapers getting a precarious living,— hardly a living. He wrote a few stories for *Putnam's Magazine*, for one of which he was paid ten dollars. One of the bright spots in this period of uncertainty was his attendance, at Springfield and Newport, upon the meetings of the American Association for the Advancement of Science. He also became more or less acquainted with men who were afterwards governors of Massachusetts, or United States senators, with John Brown and Stephen A. Douglas.

The political campaign which resulted in the election of Abraham Lincoln to the presidency is described in Mr. Coffin's own words:

"During the winter of 1859, George W. Gage, proprietor of the Tremont House at Chicago, visited Boston. I had known him many years. Being from the West, I asked him who he thought would be acceptable to the Republicans of the West as candidate for the presidency. The names prominently before the country were those of W. H. Seward, S. P. Chase, Edward Bates, and J. C. Fremont.

" ' We shall elect whomsoever we nominate,' said Mr. Gage. ' The Democratic party is going to split. The Northern and Western Democrats will go for Douglas. The slaveholders never will accept him. The Whig party is but a fragment. There will certainly be three, if not four candidates, and the Republican party can win. We think a good deal of old Abe Lincoln. He would make a strong candidate.'

"It was the first time I had heard the name of Lincoln in connection with the presidency. I knew there was such a man. Being a journalist, I had some knowledge of his debate with Douglas on the great questions of the day, but he had been defeated in his canvass for the Senate, and had dropped out of sight. It was about this time that he gave his lecture at Cooper Institute, New Haven, and Norwich. I did not meet him in Boston. His coming created no excitement. The aristocracy of Boston, including Robert C. Winthrop,

Edward Everett, George S. Hilliard, and that class, were Whigs, who did not see the trend of events. Lincoln came and went, having little recognition. The sentiment of Massachusetts Republicans was all in favor of the nomination of Seward.

"The remark of Mr. Gage in regard to Lincoln set me to thinking upon the probable outcome of the presidential contest. The enthusiasm of the Republican party was at fever heat. The party had nearly succeeded in 1856, under Fremont, and the evidences of success in 1860 multiplied, as the days for nominating a candidate approached. The disruption of the Democratic party at Charleston made the election of the Republican candidate certain.

"I determined to attend the Convention to be held at Chicago, and also that of the Whig party, to be held earlier at Baltimore.

"I visited Washington and made the acquaintance of many of the leading Republican members of Congress. Senator Wilson gave me a seat on one of the sofas in the south chamber. He was sitting by my side when Seward appeared. He stopped a moment in the passage, and leaned against the wall.

"'There is our next President,' said Wilson. 'He feels that he is to be nominated and elected.   He shows it.'

"It was evident that Mr. Seward was conscious of the expected honor.   It did not display itself in haughty actions, but in a fitting air of dignity.   He knew the galleries were looking down upon him, men were pointing him out, nodding their heads.   He was the coming man."

The Whig Convention in Baltimore, which Carleton attended, "was held in an old church from which the worshippers had departed, — a fitting place to hold it.   The people had left the Whig party, which had departed from its principles and was ready to compromise still further in slavery."

On leaving Baltimore for Chicago, and conversing with people everywhere, Carleton discovered in Pennsylvania a hostility to Seward which he had not found elsewhere.   It was geographical antagonism, New York glorying in being the Empire State, and Pennsylvania in being the Keystone of the arch.   " Pennsylvania could not endure the thought of having New York lead the procession."   Arriving in Chicago several days before the Convention opened, Carleton noticed a growing disposition to take a Western man. The contest was to be between Seward and Lincoln. On the second day the New York crowd tried to make a tremendous impression with bands and banners. Entering the building, they found it packed with the friends of Lincoln. Carleton sat at a table next to Thurlow Weed. "When the drawn ballot was taken, Weed, pale and excited, thrust his thumbs into his eyes to keep back the tears."

Mr. Coffin must tell the rest of the story:

"I accompanied the committee to Springfield to notify Lincoln of his nomination. Ashman, the president of the committee, W. D. Kelly, of Pennsylvania, Amos Jack, of New Hampshire, Sweet, of Chicago, and others made up the party. We went down the Illinois Central. It was a hot, dusty ride. Reached Springfield early in the evening. Had supper at the hotel and then called on Lincoln. His two youngest boys were on the fence in front of the house, chaffing some Democratic urchins in the street. A Douglas meeting was going on in the State House,

addressed, as I learned, by A. McClernand, —
afterwards major-general. Lincoln stood in the
parlor, dressed in black frock coat. Ashman
made the formal announcement. Lincoln's
reply was brief. He was much constrained,
but as soon as the last word was spoken he
turned to Kelly and said:

"'Judge, you are a pretty tall man. How
tall are you?'

"'Six feet two.'

"'I beat you. I'm six feet three without
my high-heeled boots on.'

"'Pennsylvania bows to Illinois, where we
have been told there were only Little Giants,'
said Kelly, gracefully alluding to Douglas, who
was called the Little Giant.

"One by one we were introduced by Mr.
Ashman. After the hand-shaking was over,
Mr. Lincoln said:

"'Mrs. Lincoln will be pleased to see you
gentlemen in the adjoining room, where you
will find some refreshments.'

"We passed into the room and were presented to Mrs. Lincoln. Her personal appearance was not remarkably prepossessing.
The prevailing fashion of the times was a

gown of voluminous proportions, over an enormous hoop. The corsage was cut somewhat low, revealing plump shoulders and bust. She wore golden bracelets. Her hair was combed low about the ears. She evidently was much gratified over the nomination, but was perfectly ladylike in her deportment.

" The only sign of refreshments visible was a white earthen pitcher filled with ice-water. Probably it was Mr. Lincoln's little joke, for the next morning I learned that his Republican neighbors had offered to furnish wines and liquor, but he would not allow them in the house; that his Democratic friends also sent round baskets of champagne, which he would not accept.

" I met him the next morning in his law office, also his secretary, J. G. Nicolay. It was a large, square room, with a plain pine table, splint-bottomed chairs, law books in a case, and several bushels of newspapers and pamphlets dumped in one corner. It had a general air of untidiness.

" During the campaign I reported many meetings for the Boston *Journal*, and was made night editor soon after Mr. Lincoln's election.

The position was very laborious and exacting.
It was the period of secession. Through the
live-long night, till nearly 3 A. M., I sat at
my desk editing the exciting news. The reporters usually left the room about eleven, and
from that time to the hour of going to press,
I was alone, — save the company of two mice
that became so friendly that they would sit on
my desk, and make a supper of crackers and
cheese, which I doled out to them. I remember them with much pleasure.

"The exacting labors and sleepless nights
told upon my health. The disturbed state
of the country made everybody in business
very cautious, so much so that the proprietor
of the *Journal*, Charles A. Rogers, began to
discharge his employees, and I was informed
that my services were no longer needed. I
had been receiving the magnificent sum of ten
dollars per week, and this princely revenue
ceased."

After President Lincoln had been inaugurated, Mr. Coffin went to Washington, during the last week in March. His experiences
there must be told by himself:

"I took lodgings at a private boarding-house on Pennsylvania Avenue, where there was a poverty-stricken Virginian, of the old Whig school, after an office. He did 'not think his State would secede.' I saw much of the Republican members of Congress, who said if I wanted a position they would do what they could for me. Senator Sumner suggested that I would make a good secretary of one of the Western territories.

" I called upon my old schoolmate Sargeant who had been for many years in the Treasury. Having constructed the telegraph fire-alarm, and done something in engineering, I thought I was competent to become an examiner in the patent office. I made out an application, which was signed by the entire Massachusetts delegation, recommending me. I dropped it into the post-office, and that was the last I saw or even thought of it, for the great crisis in the history of the country was so rapidly approaching, and so evident, that,—newspaper man as I was,—accustomed to forecast coming events, I could see what many others could not see.

" I was walking with Senator Wilson up E Street, on a bright moonlight night. The moon's rays, falling upon the unfinished dome of the Capitol, brought the building out in bold relief."

"' Will it ever be finished?' I asked. The senator stopped, and gazed upon it a moment in silence.

"' We are going to have a war, but the people of this country will not give up the Union, I think. Yet, to-day, that building, prospectively, is a pile of worthless marble.'"

Yours truly,
Charles Carleton Coffin

CHAPTER VII

WHEN the long gathering clouds broke in the storm at Sumter, and war was precipitated in a rain of blood, Charles Carleton Coffin's first question was as to his duty. He was thirty-seven years old, healthy and hearty, though not what men would usually call robust. To him who had long learned to look into the causes of things, who knew well his country's history, and who had been educated to thinking and feeling by the long debate on slavery, the Secession movement was nothing more or less than a slaveholders' conspiracy. His conviction in 1861 was the same as that held by him, when more than thirty years of reflection had passed by, that the inaugurators of the Civil War of 1861–65 were guilty of a gigantic crime.

In 1861, with his manhood and his talent, the question was not on which side duty lay,

or whether his relation to the question should
be active or passive, but just how he could
most and best give himself to the service of
his country. Whether with rifle or pen, he
would do nothing less than his best. He
inquired first at the recruiting office of the
army. He was promptly informed that on
no account could he be accepted as an active
soldier, whether private or officer, on account
of his lame heel. Rejected here, he thought
that some other department of public service
might be open to him in which he could be
more or less directly in touch with the soldiers. While uncertain as to his future course,
he was, happily for his country, led to consult
his old friend, Senator Henry Wilson, who
immediately and strenuously advised him to
give up all idea of either the army, the hospital, the clerical, or any other government
service, but to enter at once actively upon the
work of a war correspondent.

"Your talent," said Wilson, "is with the
pen, and you can do the best service by seeing what is going on and reporting it."

The author of the " Rise and Fall of the
Slave Power in America" intimated that truth,

accurately told and published throughout the North, was not only extremely valuable, but absolutely necessary. It would not take long for a thoroughly truthful reporter to make himself a national authority. The sympathizers with disunion would be only too active in spreading rumors to dishearten the upholders of the Union, and there would be need for every honest pen and voice.

After this conversation, Carleton was at peace. He would find his work and ask no other blessedness. But how to find it, and to win his place as a recognized writer on the field was a question. Within our generation, the world has learned the value of the war correspondent. He has won the spurs of the knighthood of civilization. He wears in life the laurel wreath of fame. He is respected in his calling. He goes forth as an apostle of the printed truth. The resources of wealthy corporations are behind him. His salary is not princely, but it is ample. Though he may lose limb or life, he is honored like the soldier, and after his death, the monument rises to his memory. In the great struggle between France and Germany, between Russia and Turkey, between Japan and China, and in the minor wars of European Powers against inferior civilizations, in Asia and Africa, the "war correspondent" has been a striking figure. He is not the creation of our age; but our half of this century, having greater need of him, has equipped him the most liberally. He has his permanent place of honor. If the newspaper is the Woden of our century and civilization, the war correspondent and the printer are the twin Ravens that sit upon his shoulder. The one flies afar to gather the news, the other sits at home to scatter the tidings.

In 1861 it was very different. The idea of spending large sums of money, and maintaining a staff-corps of correspondents who on land and sea should follow our armies and fleets, and utilize horse, rail car, and telegraph, boat, yacht, and steamer, without regard to expense, had not seized upon newspaper publishers in the Eastern States. Almost from the first, the great New York journals organized bureaus for the collection of news. With relays of stenographers, telegraphers, and extra printers, they were ready for all emergencies in the home office, besides liberally endowing their agencies at Washington and cities near the front, and equipping their correspondent, in camp and on deck. In this, the New England publishers were far behind those on Manhattan Island. Carleton, when in Washington, wrote his first letters to the Boston *Journal* and took the risk of their being accepted for publication. He visited the camps, forts, and places of storage of government material. He described the preparations for war and life in Washington with such spirit and graphic power, that from June 15 to July 17, 1861, no fewer than twenty-one of his letters were published in the *Journal.*

The great battle of Bull Run gave him his opportunity. As an eye-witness, his opportunity was one to be coveted. He wrote out so full, so clear, and so interesting an account, that the proprietors of the *Journal* engaged him as their regular correspondent at a salary of twenty-five dollars a week, with extra allowance for transportation. His instructions were to "keep the *Journal* at the front. Use all means for obtaining and transmitting important information, regardless of expense." This, however, was not to be interpreted to mean that he should have assistants or be the head of a bureau or relay of men, as in the case of the chief correspondent of at least three of the New York newspapers. It meant that he was to gather and transmit the news and be the whole bureau and staff in himself. Nevertheless, during most of the war, the Boston *Journal* was the only New England paper that kept a regular correspondent permanently not only in Washington, but at the seat of war. Carleton in several signal instances sent news of most important movements and victories ahead of any other Northern correspondent. He achieved a succession of what newspaper men call "beats." In those days, on account of the great expense, the telegraph was used only for summaries of news, and rarely, if ever, for long despatches or letters. The ideas and practice of newspaper managers have greatly enlarged since 1865. Entering upon his work at the very beginning of the war, he was, we believe, almost the only field correspondent who continued steadily to the end, coming out of it with unbroken health of body and mind.

How he managed to preserve his strength and enthusiasm, and to excel where so many others did well and nobly, is an open secret. In the first place, he was a man of profoundest religious faith in the Heavenly Father. Prayer was his refreshment. He renewed his strength by waiting upon God. His spirit never grew weary. In the darkest days he was able to cheer and encourage the desponding. He spoke continually, through the *Journal*, to hundreds of thousands of readers, in tones of cheer. Like a great lighthouse, with its mighty lamps ever burning and its reflectors and lenses kept clean and clear, Carleton, never discouraged, terrified, or tired out, sent across the troubled sea and through the deepest darkness the inspiriting flash of the light of truth and the steady beam of faith in the Right and its ultimate triumph. He was a missionary of cheer among the soldiers in camp and at the front. His reports of battles, and his message of comfort in times of inaction, wilted the hopes of the traitors, copperheads, cowards, and "nightshades" at home, while they put new blood in the veins of the hopeful.

Carleton was always welcome among the commanders and at headquarters. This was because of his frankness as well as his ability and his genial bonhomie and social qualities. He did not consider himself a critic of generals. He simply described. He took care to tell what he saw, or knew on good authority to be true. He did probe rumors. From the very first he became a higher critic of assertions and even of documents. He quickly learned the value of camp reports and items of news. By and by his skill became the envy of many of less experienced readers of human nature, and judges of talk and despatches. While shirking no hard work in the saddle, on foot, on the rail, or in the boat, he found by experience that by keeping near headquarters he was the better enabled to know the motions of the army as a whole, to divine the plans of the commanding general, and thus test the value of flying rumors. He had a genius for interpreting signs of movement, whether in the loading of a barge, the riding of an orderly, or the nod of a general's head. His previous training as an engineer and surveyor enabled him to foresee the strategic value of a position and to know the general course of a campaign in a particular district of country. With this power of practical foresight, he was often better able even than some of the generals to foresee and appraise results. This topographical knowledge also gave him that power of wonderful clearness in description which is the first and best quality necessary to the narrator of a series of complex movements. A battle fought in the open, like that at Gettysburg, or one of those which took place during the previous campaigns, on a plain, along the river, and in the Peninsula, is comparatively easy to describe, especially when viewed from an eminence. These battles were like those in ordinary European history; but after Grant took command of the Army of the Potomac, a reversion to something like the American colonial methods in the forest took place. The heaviest fighting was in the woods, behind entrenchments, or in regions where but little of the general scheme, and few of the operations, could be seen at once. In either case, however, as will be seen by reading over the thousand or so letters in Carleton's correspondence, his power of making a modern battle easily understood is, if not unique, at least very remarkable. With his letters often went diagrams which greatly aided his readers.

Carleton's personal courage was always equal to that of the bravest. Too sincerely appreciative of the gift of life from his Creator, he never needlessly, especially after his first eagerness for experience had been satiated, exposed himself, as the Dutch used to say, with "full-hardiness," or as we, corrupting the word, say, with "foolhardiness." He got out of the line of shells and bullets where there was no call for his presence, and when the only justification for remaining would be to gratify idle curiosity. Yet, when duty called, when there was need to know both the facts, and the truth to be deduced from the facts, whistling bullets or screeching shells never sufficed to drive him away. His coolness with pen and pencil, amid the dropping fire of the enemy, made heroes of many a soldier whose nerves were not as strong as was the instinct of his legs to run. The lady librarian of Dover, N. H., thus writes:

"An old soldier whom I was once showing through the library stopped short in front of Coffin's books and looked at them with much interest. He said that at his first battle,— I think it was Fredericksburg, but of this I am not sure, — he was scared almost to death. He was a mere boy, and when his regiment was ordered to the front and the shot was lively around him, he would have run away if he had dared. But a little distance off, he saw a man standing under the lee of a tree and writing away as coolly as if he were standing at a desk. The soldier asked who he was, and was told it was Carleton, of the *Journal*. 'There he stood,' said the man, ' perfectly unconcerned, and I felt easier every time I looked at him. Finally he finished and went off to another place. But that was his reputation among the men all through the war, — perfectly cool, and always at the front.' "

Carleton was able to withstand four years of mental strain and physical exposure because he knew and put in practice the right laws of life. His temperance in eating and drinking was habitual. Often dependent with the private soldier, while on the march and in camp, on raw pork and hardtack; helped out in emergencies with food and victuals, by the quartermaster or his assistants; not infrequently reaching the verge of starvation, he did not, when reaching city or home, play the

gourmand.   He drank no intoxicating liquor,
always politely waving aside the social glass.
He was true to his principles of total absti-
nence which had been formed in boyhood.   It
would have been easy for him to become in-
temperate, since in early boyhood he acquired
a fondness for liquors, through being allowed
to drink what might remain in the glass after
his sick mother had partaken of her tonic.
He demonstrated that man has no necessity
for alcoholic drinks, however much he may
enjoy them.

Only on one occasion was he known to taste
strong liquor.   In the Wilderness, when in a
company of officers on horseback, the blood-
curdling Confederate yells were heard but a
short distance off, and it seemed as though our
line had been broken and the day was lost for
the Union army.   At that dark moment, one
of the officers on General Meade's staff produced a flask of brandy, and remarking — with
inherited English prejudice — that he would
fortify his nerves with "Dutch courage," to
tide over the emergency, he quaffed, and then
handed the refreshment to his companion.   In
the momentary and infectious need for stimu-

lant of some sort, Mr. Coffin took a sip and handed it on. Though himself having no need of and very rarely making use of spirits, even medicinally, he was yet kindly charitable towards his weaker brethren. It is too sadly true that many of the military officers, who yielded to the temptation of temporarily bracing their nerves at critical moments, became slaves to the bottle, and afterwards confirmed drunkards. Carleton made no use of tobacco in any form.

Carleton's wonderful prescience of coming events, and his decisions rightly made as to his own whereabouts in crises, enabled him to concentrate without wasting his powers. He then gave himself to his work with all ardor, and without sparing brain or muscle, risking limb and life at Bull Run, on the Mississippi, at Fort Donelson, at Antietam and Gettysburg, in the Wilderness, at Savannah, and in Richmond. His powers in toil were prodigious. He could turn off an immense amount of work, and keep it up. When the lull followed the agony, he went home to rest and recruit, spending the time with his wife and friends, everywhere diffusing the sunshine of hope and faith. When rested and refreshed, he hied again to the front and the conflict. The careers of most army correspondents in the field were short. Carleton's race was long. His was the promise of the prophet's glorious burden in Isaiah xl. 28-31.

It was between his thirty-eighth and forty-second year, when in the high tide of his manly strength, that Carleton pursued the profession of letters amid the din of arms. His pictures show him a handsome man, with broad, open forehead and sunny complexion, standing nearly six feet high, his feet cased in the broad and comfortable boots which he always wore. Over his ordinary suit of clothing was a long and comfortable overcoat with a cape, around which was a belt, to which hung a spy-glass. Later in the war he bought a fine binocular marine glass. He gave the old "historic spy-glass" to his nephew Edmund, from under whose head it was stolen by some camp thief. In his numerous and capacious pockets, besides a watch and a pocket compass, was a store of note-books, in which he was accustomed to jot his rapid, lightning-like notes, which meant "reading without tears" for him, but woe and sorrow to those who had to knit their brows in trying to decipher his "crow-tracks." During the first part of the war he bought horses as often as he needed them, and these were not always of the first quality as to flesh or character. He usually found it difficult to recover his beast after having been away home. In the later campaigns he possessed finer animals for longer spaces of time, taking more pains, and spending more money to recover them on his return from absences North.

Nevertheless, in order to beat other correspondents, to be at the front, in the right moment, in order to satisfy the need for news, he counted neither the life nor the ownership of his horse as worth a moment's consideration. In comparison with the idea of stilling the public anxiety, and giving the news of victory, he acted upon the principle of his Master, — "Ye are of more value than many sparrows." One man, using plain English, says, " Uncle Carleton got the news, goodness knows how, but he got it always and truly. He was the cheekiest man on earth for the sake of the *Journal*, and the people of New England. He used to ask for and give news even to the commander-in-

chief.   Often the staff officers would be amazed
at the cheek of Carleton in suggesting what
should be done.   His bump of locality and
topography was well developed, and he read
the face of the country as by intuition.   He
would talk to the commander as no civilian
could or would, but Meade usually took it
pleasantly, and Grant always welcomed it, and
seemed glad to get it.   I have seen him (Grant)
in long conversations with Mr. Coffin, when
no others were near."

CHAPTER VIII

CARLETON'S account of the battle of Bull Run, where the Union forces first won the day, and then lost it through a panic, was so graphic, accurate, and comprehensive, that the readers of the Boston *Journal* at once poured in their requests that the same writer should continue his work and reports.

From his position with the Union batteries he had a fine view of the whole engagement. Many of the statements which he made were, as to their accuracy, perfect. For example, when the Confederates fired continuous volleys, making one long roll of musketry, mingled with screams, yells, and cheers, while their batteries sent a rain of shell and round shot, grape and canister, upon a body of three companies of Massachusetts men, Carleton stood with his watch in his hand to see how long these raw troops could stand such a fire. It is wonderful to read to-day his volume of "Army Correspondence," and find so little to correct.

Besides letters written on the field during the first of four battles, he wrote from Washington in review of the whole movement. He was not at all discouraged by what had happened, believing that the bitter experience, though valuable, was worth its cost. He does not seem to have been among the number of those who expected that the great insurrection would be put down in a few months. Like every one else, he was at first smitten with that glamour which the Western soldiers, led by Grant, soon learned to call " McClellanism." It was with genuine admiration that he noticed the untiring industry and superb organizing powers of " Little Mac ; " who, whatever his later faults may have been, was the man who transformed a mob of militia into that splendid machine animated by an unquailing soul, " The Army of the Potomac." Yet in the cool light of history, we must rate Gen. George B. McClellan as the military Erasmus of this war of national reformation, while Grant was its Luther.

Late in August, after ten days' rest at home to recruit exhausted energies, Carleton was once more at his post in the " City of Magnificent Distances — and big lies," attempting to draw out the truth from whole maelstroms of falsehood.   He writes: " Truly this is a city given to lying."   He had a habit of hunting down falsehoods, of tracing rumors to their holes.   Many an hour in the blazing sun, consuming his strength, did this hater of lies spend in chasing empty breaths.   Once he rode forty miles on horseback, simply to confirm or reject an assertion.   Very early, however, he learned to put every report upon the touchstone, and under the nitric acid of criticism.   He quickly gained experience, and saved much vexation to himself and his readers.   In this way his letters became what they are, like coins put in the pyx, and mintage that survives the best of the goldsmiths. When read thirty-five years after the first drying of the ink, we have a standard of truth, needing correction, for the most part, only here and there, in such details as men clearly discern only in the perspective of time.

Under McClellan's strict orders, Washington became less of a national bar-room.   The camps were made models of cleanliness, hygiene, and comfort, and schools of strict preparation for the stern work ahead.   Carleton often rode through them, and out on the picket-line. Among his other studies, being a musician, he soon learned the various notes and tones of round and conical bullet, of globular and case shot, of shell and rocket, as an Indian learns the various sounds and calls of birds and beasts.   Never wearing eye-glasses, until very late in life, and then only for reading, he was able, when standing behind or directly before a cannon, to see the missile moving as a black spot on the invisible air, and from a side view to perceive the short plug of condensed air in front of a ball, which is now clearly revealed by instantaneous photography. He soon noted how the variation in the charge of powder, and the curve of the rifle, changed the pitch of the ball, and how and why certain shells with ragged edges of lead scream like demons, and work upon the nerves by their sound and fury rather than their total of results.   He soon discovered that in a battle the artillery, except at short ranges, and in the open, bears no comparison in its killing power to the rifles of the infantry. Like an old soldier, he soon came to look with something like contempt upon the ponderous cannon and mortars, and to admire the low firing of the old veteran musket-men.

During those humiliating days, when the stars and bars waved upon Munson's Hill within sight of the Capitol, Carleton saw much of the Confederates through his glass. Picket-firing, though irregular and, probably, from a European point of view, unmilitary, trained the troops to steadiness of nerve. Many things in the first part of the war were done which were probably not afterwards often repeated; for example, the meeting of officers on the picket-lines, who had communications with each other, because they were free-masons. In September, the Confederates fell back from Munson's Hill, and on October 21st the battle at Poolsville, or Ball's Bluff, took place, in which, out of 1,800 Federals engaged, over one-third were killed, wounded or missing. The Fifteenth Massachusetts regiment suffered heavily. Colonel Devens, afterwards major-general and attorney-general, covered himself with glory, but the brave Colonel Baker lost his life.

Edward Dickinson Baker, born in England, had come to the United States in his youth. Between his thirtieth and fortieth year he had served in Congress as representative from Illinois. Then removing to California, he became a popular orator of the Republican party. In 1860 he was elected United States Senator from Oregon. I remember reading with a thrill his speech in the Senate, and his rebuke of Breckinridge. A few days later he was in Philadelphia holding a commission as colonel. He visited in their different halls the volunteer fire companies of our Quaker City. In torrents of overwhelming eloquence, he called on them to enlist in his famous "California Regiment," which was quickly clothed, equipped, and given the first rudiments of military instruction. I remember his superb, manly figure, in the very prime of life, his rosy English face set in a glory of hair just turning to silver. With hat off, he rode up and down the line, as the regiment stood in "company front" on Federal Street, between the old Cooper Shop (which was destined later to be the great Volunteers'

Refreshment Saloon) and the Baltimore Depot, where they were to take cars for the seat of war. Like the "ten thousand" with Klearchos, foreigner, but also friend and commander, of whom Xenophon in the "Anabasis" speaks, it was already uncertain whether the Philadelphia men most feared or loved their lion-hearted leader. A few weeks went by, the tragedy of Ball's Bluff took place, and in Independence Hall I saw the brave Colonel Baker's body lying in state. In that hall of heroes, it seemed to my imagination as though the painted eyes of the Revolutionary heroes looked down in sympathy and approval. There, if not already among them, soon hung also the picture of Lieutenant Henry Greble, friend and neighbor, killed at Big Bethel, and the first officer in the regular army slain during the war. Colonel, afterwards General, Charles Devens, Jr., whose acquaintance Mr. Coffin made about this time, distinguished himself from this early engagement at Ball's Bluff throughout the war, and until the closing scene at Appomattox Court House, rising to the rank of brevet major-general. Long afterwards, in Boston, having been attorney-general of the United States, I knew him as the judge of the Supreme Court of Massachusetts, meeting him socially more than once, and noticing the warm friendship between the famous war correspondent and this dignified interpreter of law.

After the battle of Ball's Bluff, seeing in detail the other and the hideous side of war in the mutilation of the human frame, and the awful horror of wounds, Carleton took a long ride through Eastern Maryland to look at the rebel batteries along the lower Potomac and to study the roads, the food products, and the black and white humanity of the Chesapeake Bay and Potomac regions, besides informing himself as to the Union flotilla. In the absence of active military operations, he wrote of the religious life of the soldiers. He was appalled at the awful profanity around him, and his constant prayer to God was for strength to resist the demoralizing influences around him, which seemed to him a hell on earth. His wife's words followed him "like a strain of music," and "the infinite purity of Jesus" was his inspiring influence.

He made himself thoroughly acquainted with the New England regiments, and studied the details in the "mosaic of the army."   He became so expert in studying the general composition of the regiments, their physical appearance, and ways of life, peculiarities of thought, speech, and action, that usually within five minutes he could tell from what State, and usually from what locality a regiment had come.   He writes:

"A regiment from Vermont is as unlike a regiment from Pennsylvania almost as a pea from a pumpkin.   Both are excellent.   Both are brave.   Both will fight well; but in the habits of life, in modes of doing a thing, they are widely different."

"Just look at the division that crosses the Potomac, and see the mosaic of McClellan's army.   Commencing on the right there is McCall's division, one grand lump of Pennsylvania coal and iron.   There is Smith's division, containing a block of Vermont marble; then Porter's tough conglomerate of Pennsylvania, New York, Michigan, Massachusetts, Maine, and Rhode Island; then McDowell's, a splendid specimen of New York; then Blenker's, a magnificent contribution from Germany, with such names as Stahl, Wurnhe, Amsburg, Bushbeck, Bahler, Steinwick, Saest, Betje, Cultes D'Utassy, Von Gilsa, and Schimmelpfennig, who talk the language of their Fatherland, sing the Rhine songs, and drink a deluge of lager beer, — slow, sure, reliable men, of the stock that stood undismayed when all things were against them, in the times of Frederick the Great, who lost everything except courage, and, that being invincible, regained all they had lost. Then there are the Irish brigades and regiments from a stock which needs no words of praise, for their deeds are written in history. Without enumerating all the divisions, we see Yankees, Germans, Irish, Scotch, Italians, Frenchmen, Norwegians, and Dutchmen, — all in one army; and, grandest spectacle of all, moved by one common impulse to put down this rebellion, and to save for all future time the principle upon which this government is founded."

Weeks and months passed, and Carleton became acquainted with all the minutiæ of camp life. He studied the peculiarities of the sutler, the army mule, the government rations, and the pies concocted in New York. He enjoyed the grand reviews, noting with his quick eye the difference, in the great host, between the volunteers and the regulars. Of the type of that noble band of officers and men, none the less patriotic because more thoroughly educated in drills than the volunteers, he wrote: " His steps are regulated, — his motions, his manners, — he is a *regular* in all these. The volunteer stoops beneath the load on his back. He is far more like Bunyan's ' Pilgrim's Progress,' with his burden of sin, than the regular. His steps are uneven, his legs are more unsteady. He carries his gun at a different angle. He lacks the finish which is obtained only by hard drill, and exact discipline." He closed this letter with a tribute of praise to Tidball's superb battery of artillery.

At this time the cavalry were not in good repute, General Scott not being in favor of any horsemen, except for scouting purposes. In this arm of the service the Confederates were far ahead of the Union soldiers. Grant, Sheridan, and Ronald McKenzie had not yet transformed our Northern horsemen into whirlwinds of fire. After various other experiences, including a long ride through Western Maryland, Carleton, within a few days before Christmas, was called by his employers to leave the Army of the Potomac, to go west to the prospective battle-field, where the heavy blows were soon to be struck.   He was succeeded in Washington by Mr. Benjamin Perley Poore.   A few noble words of farewell in his 109th letter, dated Washington, December 21, 1861, closed Carleton's first campaign in the East, his acquaintance with the Army of the Potomac having begun on the 12th of June. Having won the hearts of the soldiers in camp, and their friends at home, he left for " the next great battle-field " in the West, where, as he said, " history will soon be written in blood."   He would see how the navy, as well as the army, was to bring peace by its men of valor, and its heavy guns,— "preachers against treason."   His experience was to be of war on the waters, as well as on land.

CHAPTER IX

"HO, FOR THE GUNBOATS, HO!"

HIS first letter from the Army of the West, he dated, Cincinnati, December 28, 1861. Instead of a comparatively circumscribed Utica (on the Potomac), to confine his powers, our modern Ulysses had a line a thousand miles long, and a territory larger than several New Englands to look over. His first work, therefore, was to invite his readers to a panorama of Kentucky and the Mississippi Valley. Thus far in the war there had been no masterly moves, but, on the contrary, masterly inactivity. With such splendid chances for heroes, who would improve them? Neither Wolfe nor Washington had played Micawber, but had created opportunities. Carleton wrote, " Now is the time for the highest order of military genius. . . . We wait for him who shall improve the propitious hours." So in waiting went out the gloomy year of 1861. At Louisville, Ky., Carleton made the acquaintance in detail of General Buell's army. The commander, Don Carlos Buell, did not enjoy the presence of correspondents, and those from Cincinnati and New York papers had been expelled from the camp; nor was Carleton's letter from the Secretary of War, asking that "facilities consistent with public interests" be granted him, of any avail. He wrote on New Year's day, " No more troops are needed here, or on the Potomac at present; what is wanted is *activity*,— activity,— activity."

Following Horace Greeley's advice, Carleton went West. On January 4th, having surveyed the land and people, he sent home two letters, then moved on to Rolla, in the heart of Missouri, and, having got out of St. Louis with his passes, he found himself, January 11th, at Cairo. There the New England men were warm in their welcome of the sole representative of the press of the Eastern States, though St. Louis, Chicago, Cincinnati, and New York journals were also represented. Among these were A. D. Richardson, of the New York *Tribune*, and Whitelaw Reid, of the Cincinnati *Gazette*. Unlike General Don Carlos Buell, General U. S. Grant, in command at Cairo, had no horror of newspaper correspondents, and granted them all reasonable facilities. For the first time Carleton looked upon the gunboats, "three being of the coal-transport pattern, and five of the turtle style," with sides sloping inward, both above and below the deck. A shot from the enemy would be likely either to fly up in the air or "go into the realms of the catfish." As to the army, Carleton noticed that, as compared with the Army of the Potomac, discipline was much more severe in the East, while real democracy was much more general in the West. Men seemed less proud of their shoulder-straps. The rules of military etiquette were barely observed.

" There is but very little of the soldier about these Western troops. They are armed citizens, brave, active, energetic, with a fine physique, acquainted with hardships, reared to rough life . . . but it is by no means certain that they will not be quite as effective in the field. The troops here are a splendid set of men, all of them young. . . . There is more bone and muscle here, but less culture. . . . I

have heard far less profanity here than on the
Potomac, among officers and men." He believed there were fewer profane words used
and less whiskey drunk than among the troops
in the East. There was not as much attention
paid to neatness and camp hygiene.

It was at Cairo that Carleton made the
personal acquaintance, which he retained until
their death, of General Ulysses S. Grant and
Commodore Foote. The latter had already
made a superb reputation as a naval officer in
Africa and China. Before Foote was able to
equip and start his fleet, or Grant could move
his army southward, on what proved to be
their resistless march, Carleton made journeys
into Kentucky, wrote letters from Cincinnati
and Chicago, and arrived back in time to join
General Grant's column. He went down the
river, seeing the victorious battle and siege
operations. First from Cairo, and then from
Fort Donelson, he penned brilliant and accurate accounts of the capture of Fort Henry
and Fort Donelson, which opened the Southern Confederacy to the advance of the Union
army. While Grant beat the rebels, Carleton
beat his fellow correspondents, even though he

had first to spend many hours among the wounded. The newspaper men from New York had poked not a little fun at the "Boston man," chaffing him because they thought the New England newspapers "slow" and "out of date in methods." They fully expected that Carleton's despatches would be far behind theirs in point of time as well as in general value. Their boasting was sadly premature. Carleton beat them all, and their humiliation was great.

The matter was in this wise. He had hoped by taking the first boat from Fort Donelson to Cairo to find time to write out an account of the siege and surrender of the great fortresses; but during his travel of one hundred and eighty miles on the river, the steamer had in its cabin and staterooms two hundred maimed soldiers and officers with their wounds undressed. Instead of occupation with ink-bottle, pen, and paper, Carleton found himself giving water to the wounded, and holding the light for surgeons and nurses. Then, knowing that no other correspondent had the exact and copious information possessed by himself, he took the cars, writing his letters on the route from Cairo to Chicago, where he mailed them.

No doubt at this time, while Carleton was writing so brilliantly to a quarter of a million readers, many of them envied him his opportunities. Distance lent enchantment to the view. "But let me say," wrote Carleton, "if they were once brought into close contact with all the dreadful realities of war, — if they were obliged to stand the chances of getting their heads knocked off, or blown to atoms by an unexpected shell, or bored through with a minie ball, — to stand their chances of being captured by the enemy, — to live on bread and water, and little of it, as all of the correspondents have been obliged to do the past week, — to sleep on the ground, or on a sack of corn, or in a barn, with the wind blowing a gale, and the snow whirling in drifts, and the thermometer shrunk to zero, — and then, after the battle is over and the field won, to walk among the dying and the dead, to behold all the ghastly sights of trunkless heads and headless trunks, — to see the human form mutilated, disfigured, torn, and mangled by shot and shell, — to step in pools of blood, — to

hear all around sighs, groans, imprecations, and
prayers from dying men,—they would be content to let others become historians of the war.
But this is not all ; a correspondent must keep
ever in view the thousands that are looking
at the journal he represents, who expect his
account at the earliest possible moment.   If
he is behindhand, his occupation is gone.
His account must be first, or among the first,
or it is nothing.   Day and night he must be
on the alert, improving every opportunity and
turning it to account.   If he loses a steamboat trip, or a train of cars, or a mail, it is all
up with him.   He might as well put his pencil
in his pocket and go home."

Carleton had a hearty laugh over a letter
from a friend who advised him " to take more
time and rewrite his letters," adding that it
would be for his benefit.   To Carleton, who
often wrote amid the smoke of battle or on
deck amid bursting shells, or while flying over
the prairies at the rate of thirty-five miles an
hour, in order, first of all, to be ahead of his
rivals, this seemed a joke.   In after-years of
calm and leisure, when writing his books, he
painted word pictures and finished his chapters,

giving them a rhetorical gloss impossible when writing in haste against the pressure of rushing time. Although Boston was two hundred miles farther from Cairo than New York, yet all New England had read Carleton's account in the *Journal* before any correspondent's letters from Fort Donelson or Henry appeared in the newspapers of Manhattan.

After the fall of Columbus, the next point to which army and navy were to give attention was the famous Island Number Ten. Here the Confederates were concentrating all that were available in men and cannon. Thousands of negroes were at work upon the trenches, and it was believed that the fight would be most desperate. After long waiting for his armament and the training of his men, Commodore Foote was ready. Carleton wrote at Cairo, March 10, 1862, in the exhilaration of high hopes :

" Like the waves of the Atlantic is the tide of events. How they sweep! Henry, Donelson, Bowling Green, Nashville, Roanoke, Columbus, Hampton Roads, Manassas, Cedar Creek, — wave upon wave, dashing at the foundation of a house built upon the sand.

. . . The gigantic structure is tottering. A few more days like that of the immediate past, and the Confederacy will have a name and a place only in history. And what a history it will be! A most stupendous crime. A conspiracy unparalleled, crushed out by a free people, and the best government of all times saved to the world! How it sends one's blood through his veins to think of it! Who would not live in such an age as this? Before this reaches you, the telegraph, I hope, will have informed you that the Mississippi is open to New Orleans."

So thought Carleton then. Who at that time was wiser than he?

Island Number Ten, so named quite early in history, by the pilots descending the river, was a place but little known in the East. To the writer it was one of interest, because here had lived for a year or so a beloved sister whose letters from the plantation and home at which she was a guest were not only frequent, but full of the fun and keen interest about things as seen on a slave plantation by a bright young girl of twenty from Philadelphia. Well do I remember the handsome planter of commanding form and winning manners who had made my sister's stay in the family of the Merriwethers so pleasant, and who at our home in Philadelphia told of his life on the Mississippi. This was but two or three years before the breaking out of the war. This same plantation on Island Number Ten was afterwards sown thickly with the seed of war, shot, and shell. In front of it took place the great naval battle, which Carleton witnessed from the deck of the gunboat *Pittsburg*, which he has described not only in his letters but also in the books written later. After the destruction of the rebel fleet followed the heavy bombardment which, after many days of constant rain of iron, compelled the evacuation of the forts early in April. Even after these staggering blows at the Confederacy, Carleton expatiated on the mighty work that yet remained to be done before Secessia should become one of the curiosities of history in the limbo of things exploded.

A month of arduous toil and continuous activity on foot, on deck, and on horseback followed. On the river and in Tennessee and in Mississippi the tireless news-gatherer plied

his tasks. Then came tidings of the capture
of New Orleans, the evacuation of Fort Pillow,
in or near which Carleton wrote two of his best
letters; the retreat of the Confederates from
Memphis, and the annihilation of the rebel
fleet in a great water battle, during which
Carleton had the very best position for observation, only two other journalists being present
to witness it with him. Owing to a week's
sickness, he did not see the battle of Shiloh
or Pittsburg Landing, but he arrived on the
ground very soon after, and went over the
whole field with participants in the struggle
and while the débris was still fresh. He made
so thorough a study of this decisive field of
valor, that he was able to write with notable
power and clearness both in his letters at the
time and later in his books.

We find him in Chicago, June 17th, in Boston, June 21st, where, in one of his letters,
numbering probably about the two hundredth,
he welcomes the sweet breezes of New England,
her mountains, the deep-toned diapason of the
ever-sounding sea, the green fields, the troops
of smiling children, the toll of church bells,
and the warm grasp of hands from a host of

kind-hearted friends; and, best of all, the
pure patriotism, the true, holy devotion of
a people whose mighty hearts beat now and
ever "for union and liberty, one and insep-
arable."

CHAPTER X

THE opening of the battle-summer of 1862 found the seat of war in the East, in the tidewater region of Virginia. These were the days when "strategy" was the word. General George B. McClellan's leading idea was to capture Richmond rather than destroy the Confederate army. His own forces lay on both sides of the Chickahominy, in the peninsula below Richmond. The series of five battles had already begun when Carleton arrived in Baltimore, July 2d. A peremptory order from Washington having stopped every one from reaching Fortress Monroe, he had therefore to do the next best thing as collector and reviser of news. After studying the whole situation, he wrote a long and detailed letter from Baltimore.

Spending most of the summer at home, he was able to rejoin the army early in September, when Lee began his daring invasion of the North, — a political even more than a military move. Then Confederate audacity was fully matched by Pennsylvania's patriotism. Although the State had already one hundred and fifty regiments in service, Governor Andrew D. Curtin called for fifty thousand more men. Within ten days that number of militia were armed and equipped, and in the field. Millionaires and wage-earners, professors and students, ministers and their congregations were in line guarding the Cumberland Valley. Neither disasters nor the incapacity of generals chilled the fierce resolve of Pennsylvania's sons, who were determined to show that the North could not be successfully invaded, even by veterans led by the bravest and most competent generals of the age.

Carleton was in the saddle as soon as he learned that Lee had moved. From Parkton to Hanover Junction, to Westminster, to Harrisburg, to Green Castle, to Hagerstown, to Keitisville he rode, and at these places he wrote, hoping to be in at the mightiest battle which, until this time, had ever been fought on American soil. For many days it was a mystery to the Washington authorities, and to the Army of the Potomac, where Lee and his divisions were; but, with his usual good fortune, Carleton was but nine miles distant, at Hagerstown, when the booming of the cannon at Antietam roused him from his sleep. It was not many minutes before he was in saddle and away. Instead of the ride down the Sharpsburg pike that would have brought him in rear of the enemy, he rode down the Boonsboro road, reaching the right wing of the Union army just as Hooker was pushing his columns into position. Striking off from the main road, through fields and farms, he came to Antietam creek. He found a ford, and reached a pathway where a line of wagons loaded with the wounded was winding down the slope. On the fields above was a squadron of cavalry to hold back stragglers. In the first ambulance he descried a silver star, and saw the face of the brave General Richardson, dead, with a bullet through his breast. At the farmhouses, rows of men were already lying in the straw, waiting their turn at the surgeon's hands, while long lines of men were bringing the fallen on stretchers. With hatred of war in his heart, but with faith in its stern necessity, Carleton rode on to see the fight which raged in front of Sumner, noticing that the cannon of Hooker and Mansfield were silent, cooling their lips after the morning's fever.   Of the superb Pennsylvania Reserve Corps, which he had seen a year ago at review, there was now but a remnant.   He ascended the ridge, where thirty pieces of cannon were every moment emptying their black mouths of fire and iron.

All day long Carleton was witness of the battle, and then sent home from Sharpsburg, September 19th, in addition to his preliminary letter, a long and comprehensive account in five columns of print.   It was so animated in style, so exact in particulars, and so skilful and clear in its general grouping, that its writer was overwhelmed with congratulations by the best of all critics, his fellow correspondents.   In two other letters from Sharpsburg, he reviewed the whole subject judicially, and then returned home for a few days' recuperation.

From Philadelphia we find two of his letters, one describing the transport of troops and the monitors then on the stocks, or in the Delaware, and another reviewing the account of Antietam which he had read in the Charleston *Courier*. Indeed, all through the war, Mr. Coffin took pains to inform himself as to Southern opinion, and the methods of its manufacture and influence by the press. He was thus able to correct and purify his own judgments. He preserved his copies of the Southern papers, and gradually accumulated, during and after the war, a unique collection of the newspapers of the South. His first opinion about the battle of Antietam, written October 8, 1862, is the same as that which he held thirty years later:

"In reviewing the contest, aided by the Southern account, it seems that all through the day, complete, decisive, annihilating victory lay within our grasp, and yet we did not take it."

Let us read further from the closing paragraph of that letter, which he wrote in Philadelphia, before moving West to the army in Kentucky:

"In saying this, I raise no criticism, make no question or blame, but prefer to look upon it as a controlling of that Providence which notices the fall of every sparrow. The time had not come for complete victory, — for annihilation of the rebel army. We are not yet over the Red Sea. The baptism of blood is not yet complete. The cause of the war is not yet removed, — retribution for crime is not yet finished. We must suffer again. With firmer faith than ever in the ultimate triumph of right, truth, and justice, let us accept the fiery ordeal."

Like the pendulum of an observatory clock, the bob-point of which touches at each vibration the mercury which transmits intelligence of its movements to distant points, Carleton now swung himself to Cincinnati. In Louisville he gave an account, from reports, of the battle of Perryville. It was written in the utmost haste, with one eye upon the hands of his watch moving on to the minute of the closing of the mail. In such a case, according to his custom, he wrote a second letter, when possessed with fuller data from eye-witnesses. In the heart of Kentucky he was able to see the effects of the President's Emancipation Proclamation, which had been issued but three

weeks before.   He described the coming of
the Confederate army into Kentucky as " the
Flatterer, dressed in a white garment, who
with many fair speeches would have turned
Christian and Faithful from the glittering gates
of the Golden City, shining serene and fair
over the land of Beulah."   The robe having
dropped from Flatterer's limbs, the Kentuckian
saw that the reality was hideous, and that to
follow him was to go back again to the City of
Destruction.   The Confederates moved southward, laden with plunder, while General Buell,
with his army of one hundred and forty thousand men, after having mildly pursued them
for twenty-one days, returned to Louisville.
Carleton's comment upon these movements is,
" Such is strategy."

Finding himself again in the trough of inactivity, and ever ready to mount on the wave
of opportunity, Carleton moved again to the
East, writing in the cars while whirling to Virginia.   His first letters from the East were
penned at Harper's Ferry.   Then began his
zigzag movements, like a planet.   We find
his pen active at Berlin, Md., Purcellville, Va.,
Upperville, Va., where, beside the cavalry bat-

tles between Pleasanton and Stewart, he saw
that seven corps were in . motion. From
Gainesville, Warrenton Junction, Orleans,
Warrenton, Catlett's Station, and again and
often from Washington, and from Falmouth,
he sent his letters, which, if not always full of
battle, kept the heart of New England patient
and courageous.

McClellan had been removed, and Burnside,
taking command, led his army to the riverside
before Fredericksburg. Carleton was witness
of the bombardment of the city by the Federal
artillery. From his coign of vantage at General Sumner's headquarters, on the piazza of
an elegant mansion, one hundred feet above
the Rappahannock, and about three-quarters of
a mile from it, he could see, as though it were
a great cartoon and he a weaver of the Gobelins
tapestry of history, the awful pattern of war.
Beyond the sixteen rifled Rodman guns of
large calibre and long range, mounted on the
river bluff and thrust out through sand-bags,
behind the masses of infantry, the pontoon and
artillery trains, Carleton stood and saw the
making of a bridge in fifteen minutes, in the
face of a terrific musketry fire from the oppo-

site shore.   Then followed views of the street fight in the doomed city, the shattered houses, the cloudless sky, the setting sun, the gorgeous sunset dyes, the deepening shadows, the masses of men upon the opposite hills, the screaming shells, the puffs of white smoke, the bursting storms of iron, the blood-red flames illuminating the ruin of dwellings, the battle smoke settling in the valley, so densely as to obscure or hide the flashes.   All this was before Carleton on that afternoon and evening of that winter's day, December 11th.   Then he spread his blanket for a little sleep, expecting to awake to behold one of the greatest battles of modern times; but the sun set without the two great armies coming to close quarters.

The next day was a hard one, for Carleton was in the field until night, now watching a bombardment, now a charge, and again a long and stubborn, persistent musketry fire.   The shells sang near him, and at one time he was evidently the target for a whole Confederate battery; for, within a few seconds, a round shot struck a few rods in front of him, a second fell to the right, a third went over his head, a fourth skimmed along the surface of the ground, just over the backs of a regiment, lying flat on their faces. As he moved to the shelter of the river bank, a shot dropped obligingly in the water before him. All day long the lines of batteries on the hills smoked like Etna and Vesuvius. Sometimes, between ordnance and musketry, there were twenty thousand flashes a minute. Carleton thus far had seen no battles where the fire equalled that which was poured upon Sumner's command during the last grand, but hopeless, charge at sunset. At nightfall, when the wearied soldiers could lie down for rest, Carleton began the work of writing his letter. Among other things he said:

"With the deference to military strategics, my own common sense deprecated attempting the movements which were made, as unnecessary and unwise,—which must be accomplished with fearful slaughter, and which I believed would be unsuccessful. . . .

"It is a plain of Balaklava, where the Light Brigade, renowned in song, made their fearful charge."

Then follows a simple but sufficient diagram

of the Confederate impregnable position, where, with only common printer's type, and the "daggers" of punctuation standing for Blakesley and Armstrong guns, printer's ink told the story. Though nearly exhausted by his manifold labors of brain and muscle, Carleton, on the 15th, visited the battle-field, which did not exceed one hundred acres, and the city in which the troops were quietly quartered, but in which a Confederate shell was falling every ten minutes. After surveying the near and distant scenes from the cupola of an already well-riddled house, Carleton followed the army when it withdrew to Falmouth, seeing through his glass the Confederates leaping upon the deserted entrenchments and staring at the empty town.

Returning to Washington, he reviewed as usual the battle, and then returned homeward, according to his wont, for three weeks of rest and refreshment. His last letter, before leaving the front, was a noble and inspiriting plea for patience and continuance. He wrote: "The army is ready to fight, but the people are despondent. The army has not lost its nerve, its self-possession, its balance; it is more powerful to-day than it has ever been.   It has no thought of giving up the contest.   The cause is holy.   It is not for power or dominion, but for the rich inheritance decreed by our fathers."

The same bugle call of inspiration sounded from his lips and pen, when he rejoined the army on the Rappahannock, and Hooker was in command.   He wrote: " The army needs several things; first, to be supported by the people at home.   There is nothing which will so quickly take the strength out of the soldier as a blue letter from home, and on the other hand there is nothing which would give him so much life as a cheerful, hopeful letter from his friends. Let every one look beyond the immediate present into the years to come, and think of the inheritance he is to bequeath to his children. Let him see the coming millions of our people on this continent; let him lay his ear to the ground, and hear the tread of that mighty host which is to people the Mississippi Valley; which will climb the mountains of the West, to coin the hidden riches into gold; let him see the great cities springing up on the Pacific Coast; let him understand that this nation is yet in its youth; that this con-

tinent is to be the highway between China and
Europe; let him behold this contest in its vast
proportion, reaching through all coming time,
and affecting the entire human race forever;
let him resolve that, come weal or come woe,
come life or come death, that it shall be sustained, and it will be."

Another letter deals in rather severe sarcasm
with a friend who belonged to "the Nightshade
family," one of those individuals who thrive
on darkness. He wrote: " People of New
England, are you not ashamed of yourselves?
Away with your old womanish fears, your
shivering, your timidity, your garrulousness.
. . . Sustain your sons by bold, inspiring,
patriotic words and acts; act like men. . . .
This army, this government must be sustained.
It will be."

CHAPTER XI

AFTER five letters from Washington, in the first of which he had predicted that in a few days, for the first time in war, there would be the great contest between ironclads and forts, and the stroke of fifteen-inch shot against masonry, Carleton set off for salt water, determining to see the tug-of-war on the Atlantic coast. It was on Saturday afternoon, February 7th, that he stood on deck of the steamer *Augusta Dinsmore* as she moved through the floating masses of ice down the Hudson River to the sea. This new ship was owned by Adams's Express Company, and with her consort, *Mary Sandford*, was employed in carrying barrels of apples, boxes of clothing, messages of love, and tokens of affection between the Union soldiers along the coast and their friends at home. Heavily loaded with express packages, with fifty or sixty thousand letters, and with several hundred fifteen-inch solid shot, packed ready for delivery by Admiral Du Pont at or into Fort Sumter, the trim craft passed over a sea like glass, except that now and then was a dying groan or heave of the storm of a week before. A pleasant Sunday at sea was spent with worship, sermon, and song. After sixty hours on salt water, Carleton's ear caught the boom of the surf on the beach. The sea-gulls flitted around, and after the sun had rent the pall of fog, the town of Beaufort appeared in view.

The harbor was full of schooners which had come from up North, bringing potatoes, onions, apples, and Yankee notions for the great blue-coated community at Newburgh. Carleton moved up the poverty-stricken country through marsh, sea-sand, pitch-pine, swamp, and plain. Here and there were the shanties of sand-hillers, negro huts, and scores of long, lank, scrimped-up, razor-backed pigs of the Congo breed, as to color; but in speed, racers, outstripping the fleetest horses. Making his headquarters at Hilton Head, Carleton made a thorough study of the military and naval situation. He visited the New England regi-

ments.   He saw the enlistment of negro troops,
and devoted one letter to Colonel Thomas
Wentworth Higginson's first South Carolina
regiment of volunteers.

With his usual luck, that is, the result of
intelligence and energy which left nothing to
mere luck, Carleton stood on the steamer *Nantasket*, off Charleston, April 7, 1863.   Both
admiral and general had recognized the war
correspondents as the historians of the hour.
At half past one, the signal for sailing was dis-
played from the flag-ship.   Then the ugly
black floating fortresses moved off in a line,
each a third or a half a mile apart, against the
masses of granite at Sumter and Moultrie, and
the earthen batteries on three sides.   "There
are no clouds of canvas, no beautiful models
of marine architecture, none of the stateliness
and majesty which have marked hundreds of
great naval engagements.   There is but little
to the sight calculated to excite enthusiasm.
There are eight black specks, and one oblong
block, like so many bugs.   There are no human beings in sight, — no propelling power
visible."

A few minutes later, "the ocean boils."

Columns of spray are tossed high in air, as if a hundred submarine mines were let instantly off, or a school of whales were trying which could spout highest. There is a screaming in the air, a buzzing and humming never before so loud.

"You must think the earth's crust is ruptured, and the volcanic fires, long pent, have suddenly found vent."

"There she is, the *Weehawken*, the target of probably two hundred and fifty or three hundred guns, at close range, of the heaviest calibre rifled cannon, throwing forged bolts and steel-pointed shot turned and polished to a hair in the lathes of English workshops, advancing still, undergoing her first ordeal, a trial unparalleled in history. For fifteen minutes she meets the ordeal alone."

Soon the other four monitors follow. Seventy guns a minute are counted, followed by moments of calm, and scattering shots, but only to break out again in a prolonged roar of thunder. In the lulls of the strife, Carleton steadied his glass, and when the southwest breeze swept away the smoke, he could see "increasing pock-marks and discolorations upon the walls of the fort, as if there had been a sudden breaking out of cutaneous disease."

We now know, from the Confederate officers then in Fort Sumter, that the best artillery made in England, and the strongest powder manufactured in the Confederacy, were used during this two and a half hours of mutual hammering, until then unparalleled in the history of the world. Near sunset, at 5.20 P.M., signals from the flag-ship were read; the order was, " Retire."

The red sun sank behind the sand hills, and the silence was welcomed. During the heavy cannonade, — like the Union soldiers who, obedient to the hunter's instinct, stopped in the midst of a Wilderness battle to shoot rabbits, — a Confederate gunner had trained his rifled cannon upon the three non-combatant vessels, the *Bibb*, the *Ben Deford*, and the *Nantasket*, which lay in the North Channel at a respectful distance, but quite within easy range of Sullivan's Island. Having fired a half a dozen shot which had fallen unnoticed, the gunner demoralized the little squadron, and sent hundreds of interested spectators running, jumping, and rolling below deck, by sending a shot transversely across the *Nantasket*. It dropped in the sea about a hundred yards from the bow of the *Ben Deford*. Another shot in admirable line fell short. Shells from Cummings Point had also been tried on the ships laden with civilians, but had failed to reach them. However, the correspondents claim to have silenced the batteries, — by getting out of the way; for in a few minutes the cables had been hauled in, paddle-wheels set in motion, and distance increased from the muzzles of the battery.

When the fleet returned, Carleton leaped on board of the slush deck of the monitor *Catskill*, receiving hearty response from Captain George Rodgers, who reported " All right, nobody hurt, ready for them again." I afterwards saw all these monitors covered with indentations like spinning-top moulds or saucers. They were gouged, dented, and bruised by case-shot that had struck and glanced sidewise. Here and there, it looked as though an adamantine serpent had grooved its way over the convex iron surface, as a worm leaves the mark of its crawling in the soft earth under the stone. The *Catskill* had received thirty shots, the *Keo-*

kuk a hundred.   Inside of the *Nahant*, Carleton
found eleven officers and men badly contused
by the flying of bolt-heads in the turret; but,
except from a temporary jam, her armor was
intact.   On the *Patapsco* a ball had ripped
up the plating and pierced the work beneath.
This was the only shot that had penetrated
any of the monitors.   The *Weehawken* had
in one place the pittings of three shots which,
had they immediately followed each other,
might, like the arrows of the Earl of Douglas
in Scott's "Lady of the Lake," split each other
in twain.   Except leaving war's honorable scar,
these three bolts hurt not the *Weehawken*.
Out of probably three thousand projectiles
shot from behind walls, about three hundred
and fifty took effect, that is, one shot out of
six.   Three tons of iron were hurled at Fort
Sumter, and probably six tons at the fleet.
Fighting inside of iron towers, the Union men
had no one killed, and but one mortally
wounded.   The *Keokuk*, the most vulnerable
of all the ships engaged, sank under the northwest wind in the heavy sea of the next day.

It was long after midnight when Carleton
finished the closing lines of his letter, and then

stepped out upon the steamer's guard for a little fresh air. Over on Sumter's walls the signal-light was being waved. The black monitors lay at their anchorage. Ocean, air, and moonbeams were calm and peaceful. From the flag-ship, which the despatch steamer visited, the report was, " The engagement is to be renewed to-morrow afternoon." Nevertheless, the next day, Admiral Du Pont, dissenting from the opinions of his engineers and inspectors, as to a renewal of the attack, moreover finding his own officers differing in their opinions as to the ability of the fleet to reduce Fort Sumter, ordered no advance. The enterprise was, for the present, at least, given up. So Carleton, after another letter on white and black humanity in South Carolina, which showed convincingly the results of slavery, sailed from Hilton Head.

Like the war-horse of Hebrew poetry, he smelt the battle afar off, and looked to Virginia. He reached home just in time to hear of the great conflict at Chancellorsville. Rushing to Washington, and gathering up from all sources news of the disaster, he presented to the readers of the *Journal* a clear and connected story of the battle.   During the latter part of May and until the middle of June, the previous weeks having been times of inaction in the military world, Carleton recruited his strength at home.   Like a falcon on its perch, he awaited the opportunity to swoop on the quarry.

CHAPTER XII

WHEN Lee and his army, leaving the front of the Union army and becoming invisible, when President and people, general and chief and privates, Cabinet officers and correspondents, were wondering what had become of the rebel hosts, and when the one question in the North was, "Where is General Lee?" Carleton, divining the state of affairs, took the railway to Harrisburg. Once more he was an observer in the field. His first letter is dated June 16th, and illuminates the darkness like an electric search-light.

General Lee, showing statesmanship as well as military ability, had chosen a good time. The Federal army was losing its two years' and nine months' men. Vicksburg was about to fall. Something must be done to counterbalance this certain loss to the Confederates. Paper money in the South was worth but ten per cent. of its face value.   Recognition from Europe must be won soon, or the high tide of opportunity would ebb, nevermore to return. Like a great wave coming to its flood, the armed host of the Confederacy was moving to break at Gettysburg and recede.

Yet, at that time, who had ever thought of, or who, except the farmers and townsmen and students in the vicinity, had ever seen Gettysburg?   At first Carleton supposed that Harper's Ferry might be the scene of the coming battle.   Again he imagined it possible for Lee to move down the Kanawha, and fall upon defenceless Ohio.   He wrote from Harrisburg, from Washington, from Baltimore, from Washington again, from Baltimore once more, from Frederick, where he learned that Hooker had been superseded, and Meade, the Pennsylvanian, put in command.   On June 30th, writing from Westminster, Md., he described the rapid marching of the footsore and hungry Confederates, and the equally rapid pedestrianism of the Federals.   He revels in the splendors of nature in Southern Pennsylvania, which the Germans once hailed as a holy land of comfort and liberty, and which, by their industry,

they had made " fair as the garden of the Lord."
As Carleton rode with the second corps from
Frederick to Union Town, and thence to Westminster, he penned prose poems in description
of the glorious sight, so different from his native
and stony New Hampshire.

" The march yesterday was almost like passing through paradise. Such broad acres of
grain rustling in the breeze; the hills and
valleys, bathed in alternate sunlight and shade;
the trees so green; the air so scented with
clover-blossoms and new-made hay; the
cherry-trees ruby with ripened fruit, lining
the roadway; the hospitality of the people,
made it pleasant marching."

Thus like the great forces of the universe,
which make the ocean's breast heave to and
fro, and send the tides in ebb and flood, were
the great energies which were now to bring two
hundred thousand men in arms, on the field of
Gettysburg, in Adams County, Pennsylvania.
Forty years before, as it is said, a British officer
surveying the great plain with the ranges of
hills confronting each other from opposite sides,
with many highroads converging at this point,
declared with admiration that this would be a

superb site for a great battle.   Now the vision
of possibility was to become reality, and Carleton was to be witness of it all.   Since mid-June
he had been on the rail or in the saddle.   He
was now to spend sleepless nights and laborious
days that were to tax his physical resources to
their utmost.

With his engineer's eye, and from the heights
overlooking the main field, he took in the
whole situation.   From various points he saw
the awful battles of July 2d and 3d, which
he described in two letters, written each time
after merciful night came down upon the field
of slaughter.   He saw the charges and defeats,
the counter-charges and the continued carnage,
and the final cavalry onset made by the rebels.
He was often under fire.   An impression that
lasted all his life, and to which he often referred,
was the result of that great movement of Pick-
ett's division across the field, after the long
bombardment of the Federal forces by the Confederate artillery.   Retiring before the heavy
cannonade, Carleton had remained in the rear,
until, hearing the cheers of the Union soldiers,
he reached the slope in time to see the gray and
brown masses in the distance.

As the great wave of human life receded, that for a moment had pierced the centre of the Union forces, only to be hurled back and broken, Carleton rode out down the hill and on the plain into the wheat field. Then and there, seeing the awful débris, came the conviction that the rebellion had seen its highest tide, and that henceforth it would be only ebb.

When is a battle over, and how can one know it? That night, Friday, and the next day, Saturday, Carleton felt satisfied that Lee was in full retreat, though General Meade did not seem to think so. Carleton's face was now set Bostonwards. Not being able to use the army telegraph, he gave his first thought to reaching the railroad. The nearest point was at Westminster, twenty-eight miles distant, from which a freight-train was to leave at 4 P.M.

Rain was falling heavily, but with Whitelaw Reid as companion, Carleton rode the twenty-eight miles in two hours and a half. Covered with mud from head to foot, and soused to the skin, the two riders reached Westminster at 3.55 P.M. As the train did not immediately start, Carleton arranged for the care of his

beast, and laying his blanket on the engine's
boiler, dried it.   He then made his bed on the
floor of the bumping car, getting some sleep
of an uncertain quality before the train rolled
into Baltimore.

At the hotel on Sunday morning he was
seized by his friend, E. B. Washburn, Grant's
indefatigable supporter and afterwards Minister to France, who asked for news. Carleton
told him of victory and the retreat of Lee.
"You lie," was the impulsive answer.   Washburn's nerves had for days been under a strain.
Then, after telling more, Carleton telegraphed
a half-column of news to the *Journal* in Boston.   This message, sent thence to Washington, was the first news which President Lincoln
and the Cabinet had of Gettysburg.   After a
bath and hoped-for rest, Carleton was not
allowed to keep silence.   All day, and until
the train was entered at night for New York,
he was kept busy in telling the good news.

The rest of the story of this famous "beat,"
as newspaper men call it, is given in Carleton's
own words to a Boston reporter, a day or two
before the celebration of his golden wedding in
February, 1896:

" Monday I travelled by train to Boston, writing some of my story as I rode along, and wiring ahead to the paper what they might expect from me. When I reached the office I found Newspaper Row packed with people, just as you will see it now on election night, and every one more than anxious for details.

" It was too late, however, for anything but the morning edition of Tuesday, but the paper wired all over New England the story it would have, and the edition finally run off was a large one.

" I locked myself in a room and wrote steadily until the paper went to press, seeing no one but the men handling the copy, and, when the last sheet was done, threw myself on a pile of papers, thoroughly exhausted, and got a few hours' sleep. I went to my home in the suburbs, the next day, but my townspeople wouldn't let me rest. They came after me with a band and wagon, and I had to get out and tell the story in public again.

" The next day I left for the front again, riding forward from Westminster, where I had left my horse, and thus covering about 100 miles on horseback, and 800 miles by rail, from the time I left the army until I got back again.

"Coffee was all that kept me up during that time, but my nerves did not recover from it for a long time. In fact, I don't think I could have gone through the war as I did, had I not made it a practice to take as long a rest as possible after a big battle or engagement."

In his letter written after the decisive event of 1863, Carleton pays a strong tribute of praise to the orderly retreat which Lee made from Pennsylvania. He was bitterly disappointed that the defeated army should have been allowed to escape. With the soldiers, he looked forward with dread to another Virginia campaign. Nevertheless, he was all ready for duty. Having found his horse and resumed his saddle, he spent a day revisiting the Antietam battle-field. It was still strewn with the débris of the fight: old boots, shoes, knapsacks, belts, clothes all mouldy in the dampness of the woods. He found flattened bullets among the leaves, fragments of shells, and, sickening to the sight, here and there a skull protruding from the ground, the bleaching bones of horses and men. The Dunkers' church and the houses were rent, shattered, pierced, and pitted with the marks of war.

Even until July 15th, when he sent despatches from Sharpsburg, he nourished the hope that Lee's army could still be destroyed before reaching Richmond. This was not to be. Like salt on a sore, and rubbed in hard, Carleton's sensibilities were cut to the quick, when, on again coming home, he found the people in Boston and vicinity debating the question whether the battle of Gettysburg had been a victory for the Union army or not. Some were even inclined to consider it a defeat. Carleton's letter of July 24th, written in Boston, fairly fumes with indignation at the blind critics and in defence of the hard work of the ever faithful old Army of the Potomac, "which has had hard fighting,—terrible fighting, and little praise." He lost patience with those staying at home depreciating the army and finding fault with General Meade. He wrote: " Frankly and bluntly, I cannot appreciate such stupidity. Why not as well ask if the sun rose this morning ? That battle was the greatest of the war. It was a repulse which became a disastrous defeat to General

Lee."   He sarcastically invited critics, "instead of staying at home to weaken the army by finding fault, to step into the ranks and help do the ' bagging,' the ' cutting up,' and the ' routing ' which they thought ought to have been done."

CHAPTER XIII

AFTER the exhausting Gettysburg campaign, Carleton was obliged to rest some
weeks. So far as his letter-book shows, he did
not engage in war correspondence again until
the opening of the next year, when he entered
upon his fourth hundred of letters, and began a
tour of observation through the border States.
Traversing those between the Ohio River and
the Lakes, besides Missouri and Kansas, he
kept the *Journal* readers well informed of the
state of sentiment, and showed the preparations
made to pursue the war. At the last of April,
we find him in Washington preparing his readers for the great events of the Wilderness, in
letters which clearly describe the prospective
" valley of decision." The grandest sight, that
week, in the city, was the marching of Burnside's veteran corps, in which were not only
the bronzed white heroes, following their own

torn and pierced battle-flags, but also regiments of black patriots, slaves but a few months before, but now no longer sons of the Dark Continent, but of the Land of Hope and Opportunity. From slavery they had been redeemed in the Free Republic. Unpaid sons of toil once, but free men now, they were marching with steady step to certain victory or to certain death, for at that moment came the sickening details of the massacre of Fort Pillow. On the balcony of the hotel, standing beside the handsome Burnside, was the tall and pale man who, having given them freedom, now recognized them as soldiers. As they halted by the roadside and read the accounts of massacre, their white teeth clenched, and oaths, not altogether profane, were sworn for vengeance.

Out from the broad avenues of the nation's capital, and away from the sight of the marble dome, the great army and its faithful historians moved from sight, to the bloodiest contests of war. No more splendid pageants in the fields, but close, hard, unromantic destruction in the woods and among trenches and craters! One mind now directed all the movements of the many armies of the Union, making all the forces at the control of the nation into one mighty trip-hammer, for the crushing of Slavery's conspiracy against Liberty.

General Grant recognized in Carleton his old friend whom he first met in Cairo, and whom he had invited to take a nail-keg for a seat. Having established his reputation for absolute truthfulness, Carleton won not only Grant's personal friendship, but obtained a pass signed " U. S. Grant," which was good in all the military departments of the country, with transportation on all government trains and steamers. In hours of relaxation, Carleton was probably as familiar with Grant as was any officer on the general's own staff. Carleton profoundly honored and believed in Grant as a trained, regular army officer who could cut loose from European traditions and methods, and fight in the way required in Virginia in 1864 and 1865. Further, Grant wanted the Army of the Potomac to destroy Lee's army without the aid of, or reinforcement from, Western troops.

Carleton comprehended the magnitude of the coming campaign, in which were centred the hopes of eighteen millions of Americans. In his eyes it was the most stupendous campaign of modern times. " It is not the movement of one army merely, but of three great armies, to crush out treason, to preserve the institutions of freedom, and consolidate ourselves into a nation." Butler and Smith were to advance from the Chesapeake, the armies of the South and West were in time to march northward in Lee's rear, while from the West and North were to come fresh hosts to consummate the grand combination.

Carleton's foresight had shown him that, in this campaign, an assistant for himself would be absolutely necessary; for, in one respect, Grant's advance was unique. Instead of, as heretofore, the Union army's having its rear in close contact with the North, and all the lines and methods of communication being open, the soldiers and the correspondents were to advance into the Wilderness, and cut themselves off from the railway, the telegraph, and even the ordinary means of communication by horse, wheel, and boat. Carleton, at short notice to the young man, chose for his assistant his nephew, Edmund Carleton, now a veteran surgeon and physician in New York, but then in the freshness and fullness of youth, health, and strength.   Alert and vigorous, fertile in resource, courageous and persevering, young Carleton became the fleet messenger of the great war correspondent. He assisted to gather news, and soon learned the art of winning the soldier's heart, and of extracting, from officers and privates, scraps and items of intelligence. Even as the hunter becomes expert in noting and interpreting signs in air and on earth which yield him spoil, so young Carleton, trained by his uncle, quickly learned how to secure news, and to make a " beat."   He kept himself well supplied to the extent of his ability with tobacco, — always welcome to the veterans, for which some " would almost sell their souls ; " and with newspapers, for which officers would often give what was worth more than gold, — items of information, from which letters could be distilled, and on which prophecies could be based. Very appropriately, Carleton dedicates his fourth book on the war, " Freedom Triumphant," to his fleet messenger.

Carleton's first letter in the last long campaign is dated May 4, 1864, from Brandy Station. There four corps were assembled:

the Second, Hancock's ; the Fifth, Warren's ;
the Sixth, Sedgwick's ; the Ninth, Burnside's.
With Sheridan's riders, these made a great city
of tents.   The cavalry was not the cavalry of
Scott's day, but was in its potency a new arm
of the service.   From this time forth, the
Confederate authorities, by neglecting this arm
of their service, furnished one chief cause of
final failure, while those in Washington steadily
increased in generous recognition of the power
of union of man and horse.   In equal ability
of brute and rider to endure fatigue, the
Union cavalryman under Sheridan was a ver-
itable centaur.

While the great army lay waiting and ex-
pectant at Brandy Station, it was significant to
Carleton when the swift-riding orderlies suddenly left headquarters carrying sealed packages to the corps commanders.   First began
the tramping of the cavalry.   Next followed
the movement of two divisions of the Fifth
Corps.   All night long was heard the rumble
of artillery.   Carleton wrote : " Peering from
my window upon the shadowy landscape at
midnight, I saw the glimmering of thousands
of camp-fires, over all the plain.   Hillside,

valley, nook, and dell, threw up its flickering light. Long trains of white canvas wagons disappeared in the distant gloom.

"At three A. M., the reveille, the roll of innumerable drums, and the blow of bugles sounded, and as morning brightened, dark masses of armed men stood in long line. With the first beams of the sun peering over the landscape, they moved from the hills. Disjointed parts were welded together, regiments became brigades, brigades grew into divisions, and divisions became corps. The sunlight flashed from a hundred thousand bayonets and sabres." Thus in a few hours a great city of male inhabitants, numbering over the tenth of a million, disappeared. By night-time, in a rapid march, Grant was in headquarters in a deserted house near the Germania Ford. There Carleton noticed the general's simple style of living. Unostentatious in all his habits, he smoked constantly, often whittling a stick while thinking, and wasting no words. Grant had stolen a march upon Lee, and was as near Richmond as were the Confederates, who must attack him in flank and retard him if possible. Knowing every road and bridle-path in the Wilderness, Lee, having drawn all the resources of the Confederacy east of Georgia into his lines, had gathered an army the largest and the most complete he had yet commanded. He must now cut up Grant's host; or, if unable to do so, even without defeat, must begin a march which meant some American Saint Helena as its end.

The campaign which followed in that densely wooded part of Virginia, a few miles west of the former battle-field of Chancellorsville, had not been paralleled for hardship during the whole war. In the ten days succeeding May 4th, when the army broke camp at Culpeper and Brandy Station, there had been a march of eighteen miles, the crossing of the Rapidan with hard fighting on May 5th, and on the 6th, the great battle in the Wilderness, among the trees from which the foe could hardly be distinguished. On the 7th, there was fighting all along the line, with the night march after Spottsylvania, and on Sunday, the 8th, under the burning sun, a sharp fight by the Fifth Corps. On the 9th, another terrific battle followed, in which three corps were engaged, one of them, the Sixth, losing its noble commander, Sedgwick, with a score or two of able officers. On the 10th, in the afternoon, a pitched battle was fought all along the line, lasting until midnight, in which all the corps were engaged. On Wednesday, the 11th, skirmishing and picket firing formed the order of the day along the whole front. On Thursday, the 12th, at daybreak, the Second Corps began its attack, capturing twenty-three guns and several thousand prisoners. Sunday, the 13th, was a time of rain, hard work, hunger, and fatigue. In a word, within twelve days there had been four great pitched battles, with heavy fighting, mainly in the woods, and hard pounding on both sides, with many thousands of dead and wounded.

During the war Carleton had seen no such fighting, suffering, patience, determination. General Grant freely admitted that the fighting had been without a parallel during the war. There was little work done by the artillery. Swords and bayonets were but ornaments or emblems. Only lead had the potency of death in it. Even the cavalry dismounted, sought cover, shooting each other out of position

with their carbines.   Bullets, which do the killing, were the fixed forces.   In war it is musketry that kills, and it was a question which
side could stand murder the longest.

At the end of the Wilderness episodes, Carleton, after first answering those critics far in the
rear, who, to all the noble tenacity of Grant and
his army, queried " *Cui bono*," wrote: " I confidently expect that he [Grant] will accomplish
what he has undertaken, because he is determined, has tenacity of purpose, measures his
adversary at his true value, expects hard fighting, and prepares for it."   It was trying almost
to discouragement, to this brave, honest, patient seeker after truth, to find with what chaff
and husk of imaginary news, manufactured
in Washington and elsewhere, the editors of
newspapers had to satisfy the hungry souls of
the waiting ones at home.

In one of the engagements, when our right
wing had been forced by the Confederates;
when the loud rebel yells were heard so near
that the teamsters of the Sixth Corps were
frightened into a panic, and, cutting the traces,
ran so far and wide that it was two days before
they were got together again; when, to many

army officers, it seemed the day had been lost,
— as lost it had been, save for the stubborn
valor of the Sixth Corps; when many a face
blanched, Carleton looked at Grant.   There
was the modern Silent One, tranquil amid the
waves of battle.   Sitting quietly, with perfect
poise, eyes on the ground, and steadily smoking, he whittled a stick, neither flesh nor spirit
quailing.   "He himself knew what he would
do."   And he did wait, and, in waiting, won.
Carleton's faith in Grant, strong from the first,
was now as a mountain, unshakable.

CHAPTER XIV

CAMP LIFE AND NEWS-GATHERING

THE story of the Wilderness campaign, during which were fought the greatest musketry battles in the history of the world, with their awful slaughter, has been told by hundreds of witnesses, and by Carleton himself in his books; but the life of the camp and how the great army was handled, how the news was forwarded, and how Carleton beat the government couriers and all his fellow historians of the hour, getting the true report of the awful struggle before the country, has not been told, or at least, only in part. Let us try to recall some of the incidents.

In the first place, this was the time of the year when the flies and manifold sort of vermin, flying, crawling, hopping, hungry, and ever biting, were in the full rampancy of their young vigor. It was not only spiteful enemies in human form, that sent crashing shells and piercing bullets, but every kind of nipping, boring, sucking, and stinging creatures in the air and on the earth, that our brave soldiers, and especially our wounded, had to face. Even to the swallowing of a mouthful of coffee, or the biting of a piece of hard tack, it was a battle. Flies, above, around, and everywhere, made it difficult to eat without taking in vermin also. Even upon the most careful man, the growth of parasites in the clothing or upon the person was a certainty. Within twenty-four hours the carcass of a horse, left on the field of battle, seemed to move with new and multitudinous life suddenly generated. The stench of the great battle-fields was unspeakable, and the sudden creation of incalculable hosts of insects to do nature's scavenger work was a phenomenon necessary, but to human nerves horrible. The turkey-buzzards gathered in clouds for their hideous banquet.

All this made the work of the surgeons greater, and the sufferings of the wounded more intense; yet, redeeming the awful sight of torn and mangled humanity, was the splendid discipline and order of the medical staff. Upon the first indications of a battle, the regi-

mental wagons of each corps would be driven
up to some real or supposed safe place. It
was the work of but a few moments for the
tables to be spread with all their terrible array
of steel instruments, while close at hand would
be the stores of lint, bandages, towels, basins,
and all the paraphernalia which science and
long experience had devised. These diminished, in some measure, the horrors of the
battle for at least the wounded. It was a sublime and beautiful sight, as compared with the
wars of even a century ago, when the surgeon
had scarcely a recognized position in the army.
In the very midst of the hell of fire and flame
and noise, the relief parties, with their stretchers,
would go out and return with their burdens.
Soon the neighborhood of the surgeon's wagon
looked like a harvest-field with the windrows
of cut grain upon it. Strange as it may seem,
there was often more real danger in this going
and coming from rear to front, and from front
to rear, than on the very battle line itself.
Many a man preferred to stand in the fighting
files with the excitement and glory, than to get
out into the uncertain regions of wandering
balls and bursting shells. The Carletons, both

uncle and nephew, had often, while out collecting news, to scud from cover to cover, and amid the " zip, zip " of bullets. Dangerous as the service was, there was little reward to the eyesight, for the Confederate army, like the Japanese dragon of art, was to be seen only in bits, here and there.

How easy for us now, in the leisure of abundant time and with all the fresh light that science has shed upon surgery, and focussed upon the subject of gunshot wounds, to criticise the surgeons of that day, who, with hundreds of men each awaiting in agony his turn, were obliged to decide within minutes, yea, even seconds, upon a serious operation, without previous preparation or reinforcement of the patient. The amputation, the incision, the probing had to be done then and there, on the instant. It is even wonderful that the surgeons did as well as they did. Often it was a matter of quick decision as to whether anything should be attempted. One look at many a case was enough to decide that death was too near. Often the man died in the stretcher; sometimes, when marked for the operating-table, he was asleep in his last sleep before his turn came. Surgeons, hospital stewards, nurses, detailed men, had to concentrate into moments what in ordinary hospital routine may require hours.

Human nature was reduced to its lowest terms when hunger made the possessors of a stomach forget whether they were men or wolves. The heat was so intense, the marching so severe, that many of the men would throw away blankets, rations, and equipments, and then make up in camp by stealing. Severe punishment was meted out when ammunition was thrown away. The débris on the line of march, and the waste, was tremendous. Only strict military discipline made property respected. Even then, the new conscript had to look out for his bright and serviceable musket when the old veteran's arms were lost or out of order. The newspaper correspondent owning a good horse had to keep watch and ward, while so many dismounted cavalrymen whose horses had been shot were as restless as fish out of water. It was hard enough even for the soldiers to get rations during the Wilderness campaign, harder often for the men of letters. Had it not been for kind quartermasters, and the ability of the correspondents to find the soft side of their hearts, they must have starved. Yet the rapidity with which soldiers on their forced marches could turn fences into fires and coffee into a blood-warmer was amazing. The whole process from cold rails to hot coffee inside the stomach often occupied less than twenty minutes. In these "ramrod days," "pork roasts" — slices of bacon warmed in the flame or toasted over the red coals — made, with hard tack, a delicious breakfast.

Once when the Second Corps had captured several thousand Confederate prisoners, who were corralled in an open field in order to be safely guarded, and their commander brought into the presence of General Grant, the former remarked that his men had had nothing to eat for the past twenty-four hours. Instantly Grant gave the order for several wagon-loads of crackers to be brought up and distributed to the hungry. Thereupon appeared a spectacle that powerfully impressed young Carleton. The six-muled teams appeared in a few moments and were whipped up alongside of the Virginia rail fence. Then the stalwart teamsters, aided by some of the boys in blue, stood beside the wagons to distribute boxes. Two men, taking each the end of a box in hand, after two or three preparatory swings, heaved the box full of biscuit up in the air and off into the field. Within the observation of young Carleton, no box, while full, ever reached the ground, but was seized while yet in the air, gripped and ripped open by the men that waited like hungry wolves. They tore open the packed rows of crackers and fairly jammed them down their famished mouths, breaking up the hard pieces in their hands while waiting for their teeth to do its hasty work. Humanity at its noblest, in Grant's instantly ordering food, and in its most animal phase of necessity, in the hungry rebels devouring sustenance, were illustrated on that day.

After work with the pen concerning the great battles in the Wilderness, Carleton's great question was how to get his letters to Boston. The first bundle was carried by Mr. Wing, of the New York *Tribune*, the second by Mr. Coffin's nephew, Edmund Carleton. The nearest point occupied by the Union army, which had communication with the

North by either boat, mail or telegraph, was Fredericksburg, more than forty miles to the eastward. To reach this place one must ride through a region liable at any moment to be crossed by regular Confederate cavalry, Mosby's troops, or rebel partisans. There were here and there outposts of the Union cavalry, but the danger to a small armed party, and much more to a single civilian rider, was very great. Nevertheless, young Carleton was given his uncle's letters, with the injunction to ride his horse so as not to kill it before reaching Fredericksburg. "The horse's life is of no importance, compared with the relief of our friends' anxiety; and, if necessary to secure your purpose of prompt delivery, let the horse die, but preserve its life if you can."

To make success as near to certainty as possible, young Carleton took counsel with the oldest and wisest cavalrymen. He then concluded to take the advice of one, who told him to give his horse a pint of corn for breakfast and allow the animal plenty of time to eat and chew the fodder well. Then, during the day, let the beast have all the water he wanted, but no food till he reached his destination. Fortunately, his horse, being "lean," was the one foreordained in the proverb for the "long race." The young messenger lay down at night with his despatches within his bosom, his saddle under his head, and his horse near him. The bridle was fastened around his person, and all his property so secured that the only thing that could be stolen from him without his being awakened was his hat and haversack, — though this last was under his saddle-pillow. Nothing else was loose.

The young man rose early. Alas! he had been bereaved indeed. Not only his hat, but his haversack, with all toilet articles, his uncle's historic spy-glass, and his personal notes of the campaign, were gone. While his horse chewed its corn he found a soldier's cap, vastly too small, but by ripping up the back seam he was able to keep it on his head and save himself from sunstroke. Mounting his horse, he set out eastward at sunrise. When some miles beyond the Federal lines, he was challenged by horsemen whom he found to be of the 13th Pennsylvania cavalry on outpost duty and just in from a foraging trip. They hesitated to release him even after examining his passes, but "that from Butler fetched them." Even then, they did not like him to proceed, assuring him that it was too dangerous for anybody to cross such unprotected territory. He would be "a dead man inside of an hour." However, they examined his horse's shoes, and gave him a strip of raw pork, the first food he had tasted for many an hour. Finally they bade him good-by, promising him that he was going " immediately to the devil." Some miles further on, he saw near him two riders. Mutually suspicious of each other, the distance was shortened between the two parties until the character of each was made known. Then it was discovered that all three were on the same errand, the solitary horseman for Boston private enterprise, and the two cavalrymen in blue for General Grant to the Government, were conveying news.

They rode pleasantly together for a few minutes, but when Carleton noticed that their horses were fat and too well-fed to go very fast, he bade his companions good-by. He put spurs to his horse. Though it was the hottest day of the year, he reached Fredericksburg about the middle of the forenoon, thirsty

and hungry, having eaten only the generous
cavalryman's slice of raw pork on the way.
He found there a train loading with the
wounded of several days' battle. He at once
began helping to carry the men on the cars.
Volunteering as a nurse, where nurses were
most needed, though at first refused by the
surgeons, he got on board the train. From
the Sanitary Commission officers, he received
the first "square meal" eaten for many days.
At Acquia Creek, he took the steamboat, and
after helping to transfer the wounded from
cars to boat, he remained on board, sleeping
on a railing seat. Next morning he was in
Washington, before the newspaper bureaus
were open.

He sent by wire a brief account of the Wilderness battles. At first the operator was
very reluctant to transmit the message, since
he was sure that none had been received by
the Government, and he feared reprimand or
discharge for sending false reports. Indeed,
this information sent by Carleton was the first
news which either President Lincoln or Secretary Stanton had of Grant's latest movements.

From the telegraph office, young Carleton

went to the Boston *Journal* Bureau, on 14th Street.   There he had to wait some time, since Mr. Coffin's successor in Washington, not expecting any tidings, was leisurely in appearing.   By the first mail going out, however, a " great wad of manuscript," put in envelopes as letters, was posted.   Again the *Journal* beat even the official messengers and the other newspapers in giving the truthful reports of an eye-witness.   Thus, Charles Carleton Coffin scored another triumph.

How to get back to the army was now a question for young Carleton.   The orders of the Secretary of War were peremptory that no one should leave Washington for the front. The correspondents who were there might stay, but no fresh accessions could be made to the ranks of the news-gatherers.   How, then, could young Carleton pierce through the hedge of authority ?

But the man diligent in business shall stand before kings.   Young Carleton, securing a commission as nurse from Surgeon-General Hammond, went down to the riverside, and, going on board a steamer arriving with wounded, he helped to unload its human

freight.   When the last man had been carried
over the gunwales, young Carleton stayed on
board.   When far down the river, on the returning boat, he ceased being something like a
stowaway, and became visible.   No one challenged or disturbed him.   At Acquia Creek,
he found that General Augur, having sent all
his wounded North, was just abandoning the
communication.   Young Carleton then went
to Belle Plain, and thence marched three days
with three companies of the Veteran Invalid
Corps, and rejoined the army on its forced
march, when Grant moved by the left flank
down towards Petersburg.

Meanwhile, the pride of Mr. Coffin, the
journalist, and the conscience of Mr. Coffin,
the man, the uncle, and the Christian, had
been at civil war.   He was berating himself
for having let his nephew go on so dangerous
an errand.   When the news flew round the
camp that " young Carleton's back," Mr. Coffin rushed up to his nephew, wrung his hand,
and cried out, with beaming face, " Ed, you're
a brick."

CHAPTER XV

BY this time, Mr. Coffin was himself nearly
exhausted, having been worn down by
constant service, day and night, in one of the
most exhausting campaigns on record. Knowing that both armies would have to throw up
entrenchments and recuperate, he came home,
according to custom, to rest and freshen for
renewed exertion. Leaving immediately after
the battle of Cold Harbor, that is, on June
7th, he was back again in Washington on
June 22d, and in Petersburg, June 26th. The
lines of offence and defence were now twenty
miles long, and the great battle of Petersburg,
which was to last many months, the war of
shovel and spade, had begun. Mr. Coffin
remained with the army, often riding to City
Point and along the whole front of the Union
lines, reading the news of the sinking of the
Alabama by the *Kearsarge*, and the call of the

President for a half million of men, seeing many of the minor contests, the picket firing, the artillery duels, and learning of the splendid valor of the black troops.

He came to Washington and Baltimore, when the news of Early's raid up the Shenandoah Valley was magnified into an invasion of Maryland by General Lee, with sixty thousand men behind them. Carleton, however, was not one to catch the disease of fear through infectious excitement. Finding Grant, the commander-in-chief of all the armies in the field, walking alone, quietly and unostentatiously, with his thumbs in the armholes of his vest, and smoking a cigar, neither excited nor disturbed, Carleton felt sure that the raid had been anticipated and was well provided for. Both then, as well as on July 18th, when he had to argue with friends who wore metaphorically blue glasses, he wrote cheerfully and convincingly of his calm, deliberate judgment, that the prospects of crushing the rebellion were never so bright as at that moment. He concluded his letter thus, "Give Grant the troops he needs now, and this gigantic struggle will speedily come to an end."

While Lee, disappointed in the results of
Early's menace of Washington, was summon-
ing all his resources to resist the long siege,
and while Grant was awaiting his reinforce-
ments and preparing the cordon, which, like a
perfect machine, should at the right moment be
set in motion to grind in pieces the armies of
rebellion, Carleton was chosen by the people
of Boston to accompany their gift of food
which they wished to send to Savannah, to relieve the needy. Between Tuesday and Thursday of one week, thirty thousand dollars were
contributed. The steamer *Greyhound*, a captured blockade-runner, was chartered. Taking
in her hold one-half of the provisions, she left
Boston Harbor at 3 o'clock on Saturday afternoon, January 23, 1865. With the committee
of relief, Carleton arrived in Savannah in time
to ride out and meet the army of Sherman.
After attending meetings of the citizens, seeing
to the distribution of supplies, and writing a
number of letters, he now scanned all horizons,
feeling rather than seeing the signs of supreme
activity. Whither should he go?

Sherman's army was about to move north
to crush Johnston, and then join Grant in de-

molishing Lee's host.   Mr. Coffin could easily
have accompanied this marvellous modern
Anabasis, which, however, instead of retreat
meant victory.   He had an especially warm
invitation from Major-General A. S. Williams,
commander of the 20th Corps, to be a guest
at his headquarters.   There were many arguments to tempt him to proceed with Sherman's
army.   Nevertheless, from the war correspondent's point of view, it seemed wiser not to go
overland, but to choose the more unstable
element, water.   For nearly a month, perhaps
more, the army would have no communication
with any telegraph office, and for long intervals
none with the seacoast.

Carleton knew that after Gilmore's "swamp
angel" and investing forces had done their
work, Charleston must soon be empty.   He
longed to see the old flag wave once more
over Sumter.   So, bidding farewell to Sherman's army, he took the steamer *Fulton* at
Port Royal, which was to stop on her way to
New York at the blockading fleet off Charleston.   Happy choice!   He arrived in the nick
of time, just as the stars and stripes were being
hoisted over Sumter.   It was on February

18th, at 2 P. M., that the *Arago* steamed into Charleston Bay, where he had before seen the heaviest artillery duel then known in the history of the world, and the abandonment of the attack by the floating fortresses. Now a new glory rose above the fort, while in the distance rolled black clouds of smoke, from the conflagration of the city. He penned this telegram to the Boston *Journal :*

" The old flag waves over Sumter, Moultrie, and the city of Charleston.

" I can see its crimson stripes and fadeless stars waving in the warm sunlight of this glorious day.

" Thanks be to God who giveth us the victory."

Carleton had but a few minutes to write out his story, for the steamer *Fulton* was all ready to move North. How to get the glorious news home, and be first torch-bearer in the race that would flash joy over all the North, was now Carleton's strenuous thought. As matter of fact, this time again, as on several occasions before, he beat the Government and its official despatch-bearers, and all his fellow correspondents.

How did he do it?

While other knights of the pen confided their missives to the purser of the despatch steamer, *Arago*, Carleton put his in the hands of a passing stranger, who was going North. Explaining to him the supreme importance of rapidity in delivery of such important news, he instructed him as follows:

"When your steamer comes close to the wharf in New York, it will very probably touch and then rebound before she is fast to her moorings. Do you stand ready on the gunwale, and when the sides of the vessel first touch the dock, do not wait for the rebound; but jump ashore, and run as for your life to the telegraph office, send the telegram, and then drop this letter in the post-office."

Carleton's friend did as he was told. He watched his opportunity. In spite of efforts to hold him back, he was on terra firma many minutes before even the Government messenger left the boat; while, unfortunately for the New York newspapers, the purser kept the various correspondents' despatches in his pocket until his own affairs had been attended to. It was about 8 o'clock in the morning when

Carleton's messenger faced the telegraph operators. Then, as Carleton told the story in 1896, " they at first refused to take the story, as they did not believe its truth, and said it would affect the price of gold. In those days, there was a censorship of the telegraph, and nothing was allowed to be sent which might affect the price of gold.

" But finally they sent the story, and it was bulletined in Boston and created a great sensation. It was wired back to New York and pronounced a canard by the papers there, since the steamer from Charleston was in and they had no news from her.

" They were set right, though, when about noon the purser, having finished his own work, delivered the stories entrusted to him."

The despatch, which was received in the *Journal* office soon after 9 o'clock A. M., was issued as an extra, containing about sixty-five lines, giving the outline of the great series of events. This telegram was the first intimation that President Lincoln and the Cabinet at Washington received of the glorious news. Being signed "Carleton," its truth was assured.

The next day, in the city " where Secession

had its birth," Carleton walked amid the
burning houses and the streets deserted of its
citizens, saw the entrance of the black troops,
and went into the empty slave-market, securing. its dingy flag — the advertisement of sale
of human bodies — as a relic.   During several
days he wrote letters, in which the notes of
gratitude and exultation, mingled with pity
and sympathy with the suffering, and full of
scarcely restrainable joy in view of the speedy
termination of the war, are discernible.

CHAPTER XVI

WITH LINCOLN IN RICHMOND.

WHITHER now should Carleton go? There were but few fields to conquer, for the slaveholders' rebellion was swiftly nearing its end, and Carleton felt his work with armies and amid war would soon and happily be over. He knew it was now time for Grant to deliver his blows, and make the anvil at Petersburg ring. Eager to be in at the death of treason, he hastened home, shortened his stay with wife and friends, and hurried on to City Point. As usual, he was present in the nick of time. He was able to write his first letter from the Army of the Potomac, descriptive of the attack on Fort Steadman, March 25th. On the 26th he saw again the sparkling-eyed Sheridan. Once more he began to use his whip of scorpions upon the editors and people who were bestowing all praises upon the Army of the West, with only

criticism or niggardly commendation for the
Armies of the Potomac and the James, with
many a sneer and odious comparison. He
witnessed the tremendous attack of the rebel
host upon the Ninth Corps, hearing first the
signal gun, next the rebel yell, then the rat-
tling fire of musketry deepening into volleys,
and finally the roar of the cannonade. Carleton, within three minutes after the firing of the
first gun, took position with his glass and note-
book, upon a hill. One hundred guns and
mortars were in full play, surpassing in beauty
and grandeur all other night scenes ever witnessed by him. In some moments he could
count thirty shells at once in the air, which
was filled with fiery arcs crossing each other
at all angles. Between the flaming bases, at the
muzzle and the explosion, making two ends of
an arch, there were thousands of muskets
flashing over the entrenchments. Yet, despite
the awful noise and the spectacle so magnificent to the eye, there were few men hurt
within the Union lines.

After forty hours of rain, the wind blew
from the northwest, and the mud rapidly disappeared. Then Carleton began to look out

for the great event, in which such giants as Lee and Johnston on one hand, and Grant, Sherman, Sheridan, Thomas, and Hancock on the other, were to finish the game of military mathematics which had been progressing during four years. Carleton wrote, March 31, 1865, "How inspiring to watch the close of such a game." He expected a great battle. "The last flicker of a candle is sometimes its brightest flame."

He was not disappointed. On mid-afternoon of April 1st, Carleton was at Sheridan's headquarters witnessing the battle of Five Forks, and the awful bombardment of Saturday night. Then went out Grant's order to "attack along the whole line." Now began the bayonet war. At 4 o'clock on that eventful Sunday, like a great tidal wave, the Union Army rolled over the rebel entrenchments. This is the way Carleton describes it in *Putnam's Magazine* :

"Lee attempted to retrieve the disaster on Saturday by depleting his left and centre, to reinforce his right. Then came the order from Grant, 'Attack vigorously all along the line.' How splendidly it was executed! The

Ninth, the Sixth, the Second, the Twenty-fourth Corps, all went tumbling in upon the enemy's works, like breakers upon the beach, tearing away chevaux-de-frise, rushing into the ditches, sweeping over the embankments, and dashing through the embrasures of the forts. In an hour the C. S. A., — the Confederate *Slave Argosy*, — the Ship of State launched but four years ago, which went proudly sailing, with the death's-head and cross-bones at her truck, on a cruise against Civilization and Christianity, hailed as a rightful belligerent, furnished with guns, ammunition, provisions, and all needful supplies, by England and France, was thrown a helpless wreck upon the shores of time."

On April 2d, he wrote from Petersburg Heights telling of the movements of Sheridan's cavalry and the Ninth, Second, and Twenty-fourth Corps.

On the 3d, he was in Richmond, writing, " There is no longer a Confederacy."

He had been awakened by the roar of the Confederate blowing up of ironclads in the James River. A few minutes later he was in the Petersburg entrenchments. He rode solitary and lone from City Point to Richmond, entering the city by the Newmarket road, and overtaking a division of the Twenty-fifth Corps. Dismounting at the Spottswood House, he registered his name on the hotel book, so thickly written with the names of Confederate generals, as the first guest from a "foreign country," the United States. The clerk bade him choose any room, and even the whole house, adding that he would probably be burned out in a few minutes. Parts of the city had already become a sea of flame, but Richmond was saved, and the fire put out by Union troops. Military order soon reigned, and plundering was stopped. He met President Lincoln, and helped to escort him through the streets lined with the black people whom he had set free. Later, Carleton saw and talked with Generals Weitzel and Devens in the capitol, shaking hands also with Admiral Farragut. From the top of the capitol building, he reflected on the fall of Secession. He saw Libby Prison inside and out, as well as the old slave-mart, holding the key of the slave-pen in his hand. He has told the story of his Richmond experiences in

lectures, magazine articles, and in his book,
" Freedom Triumphant." His verbal descriptions enabled Thomas Nast to paint his
famous picture of Lincoln in Richmond.

Carleton's last letter, completing his war
correspondence, is dated April 12th, 1865.
It depicts the scene of the surrender, thus
completing a series of about four hundred
epistles, not counting the ten or a dozen lost
in transmission. In these he not only wrote
history and furnished material for it, but he
kept in cheer the heart of the nation.

Finally the great rebellion was crushed by
the navy and army. Foote, Farragut, Dupont,
and Porter, with their men on blockade and
battle-deck duty, made possible the victories
of Grant, Thomas, Sheridan, and Sherman.
Carleton as witness and historian on the ships,
in water fresh and salt, as well as in the camps
and field, appreciated both arms of the service.
His letters were read by thousands far beyond
the Eastern States, and often his telegrams
were the only voice crying out of the wilderness of suspense, and first heard at Washington and throughout the country, proclaiming
victory.

CHAPTER XVII

AFTER four years of strenuous activity of body and brain, it was not easy for Carleton to settle down at once to commonplace routine. Having exerted every nerve and feeling in so glorious a cause as our nation's salvation, every other cause and question seemed trivial in comparison. Succeeding such a series of excitements, it was difficult to lessen the momentum of mind and nerve in order to live, just like other plain people, quietly at home. One could not be drinking strong coffee all the time, nor could battle shocks come any longer every few weeks. The sudden collapse of the Confederacy, and the ending of the war, was like clapping the air-brakes instantaneously upon the Empire State Express while at full speed. While the air pressure might stop the wheels, there was danger of throwing the cars off their trucks.

It took Carleton many months, and then only after strong exertion of the will, careful study of his diet and physical habits, to get down to the ordinary jog-trot of life and enjoy the commonplace. He occupied himself during the latter part of 1865 in completing his first book, which he entitled " My Days and Nights upon the Battle Field." This was meant to be one in a series of three volumes. He had written most of this, his first book, in camp and on the field. In form, it was an illustrated duodecimo of 312 pages, and was published by Ticknor and Fields, and later republished by Estes and Lauriat.

It carries the story of the war, and of Carleton's personal participation in it in the Potomac and Mississippi River regions, down to the fall of Memphis in the summer of 1862.

After this, followed another volume, entitled " Four Years of Fighting," full of personal observation in the army and navy, from the first battle of Bull Run to the fall of Richmond. This was a more ambitious work, of five hundred and fifty-eight, with an introduction of fifteen, pages. It contained a portrait and figure of the war correspondent, with pencil and note-book in hand. Published by Ticknor and Fields, it was reissued in 1882, by Estes and Lauriat, under the title of "Boys of '61." Carleton completed a careful revision of this work about a fortnight before his golden wedding, for another edition which appeared posthumously in October, 1896.

Meanwhile, Mr. Coffin had reëntered the work of journalism in Boston. This, with his books and public engagements, as a lecturer and platform speaker, occupied him fully. In the summer of 1866 the shadows of coming events in Europe began to loom above the horizon of the future. The great Reform movement in England was in progress. The triumph of the American war for internal freedom, the vindication of Union against the pretensions of State sovereignty, the release of four million slaves, the implied honor put upon work, as against those who despised workmen as "mudsills," had had a powerful reaction upon the people of Great Britain. These now clamored for the rights of man, as against privileged men. British liberty was once more "to broaden down from precedent to precedent." In France, the World's Exposition was being held. Prussia and Austria had rushed to arms.

The evolution of a modern German empire had begun. Austria and Hungary were being drawn together. Should Prussia humble her Austrian foe, then Italy would throw off the yoke, and the Italians, once more united as a nation, would see the temporal power of the Pope vanish. Victor Emmanuel's troops would enter Venice and perhaps even the Eternal City.

To tell the story of storm and calm, of war and peace, Carleton was again summoned by the proprietors of the Boston *Journal*, and at a salary double that received during the war. This time his wife accompanied him, to aid him in his work and to share his pleasure. On one of the hottest days of the summer, they sailed on the Cunard steamer *Persia*, from New York. This was to be Carleton's first introduction to a foreign land. The chief topic of conversation during the voyage was the Austro-Prussian War, which, it was generally believed, would involve all Europe. The storm-cloud seemed to be vast and appalling.

They arrived in Liverpool, the cloud had

burst and disappeared, and the sky was blue
again.   The battle of Sadowa had been fought.
Prussian valor and discipline in handling the
needle-gun had won on the field.   Bismarck
and diplomacy were soon to settle terms of
peace, and change the map of Europe.

Carleton hastened on to London to hear the
debate in Parliament on the extension of the
suffrage, to see the uprising of the people, and
to notice how profoundly the great struggle in
America and its results had affected the English people.   Great Britain's millions were de-
manding cheaper government, without so many
costly figureheads, both temporal and spiritual, and manhood suffrage.   The long period
of nearly constant war from 1688 to 1830 had
passed.   In area of peace, men were thinking
of, and discussing openly, the relation of the
middle classes and the laboring men to the
nobility and landed estates.   Agitated crowds
thronged the streets, singing " John Brown's
Soul is Marching on."

Mr. Gladstone's bill was defeated.   Earl
Russell was swept out of office, and Disraeli
was made chancellor.   It was a field-day in
the House of Commons when Carleton heard

Gladstone, Bright, Lowe, and the Conservative and Liberal leaders. These were the days when such men as Governor Eyre, after incarnating the most brutish principle of that worse England, which every American and friend of humanity hates, could be defended, lauded, and glorified. Indeed, Eyre's bloody policy in Jamaica was approved of by such men as John Ruskin, Charles Kingsley, and other literary men, to the surprise and pain of Americans who had read their books. On the other hand, the men of science and thinking people in the middle and laboring classes condemned the red-handed apostle of British brutishness. All through this, his first journey in Great Britain, as in other countries years afterward, Carleton clearly distinguished between the Great Britain which we love, and the Great Britain which we do not love, — the one standing for righteousness, freedom, and progress; the other allied with cruelty, injustice, and bigotry.

After studying British finance, political corruption, the army, and the system of purchasing commissions then in vogue, and visiting the homes of the Pilgrims in Lincolnshire,

and the county fairs, the land of Burns, and
the manufactures of Scotland, Carleton turned
his face towards Paris. Before leaving the
home land of his fathers, he dined and spent
an afternoon with the great commoner, John
Bright. Mrs. Coffin accompanied him and
enjoyed Mrs. Bright, who was as modest,
unassuming, kind, and genial as her husband.
John Bright listened with intense interest and
profound emotion to Carleton's personal reminiscences of Mr. Lincoln, and of his entrance
into Richmond. Before leaving for France,
on the 5th of September, Carleton wrote:

" The thunder of Gettysburg is shaking the
thrones of Europe. English workmen give
cheers for the United States. The people of
Germany demand unity. Louis Napoleon, to
whom Maximilian had said, ' Mexico and the
Confederacy are two cherries on one stalk,'
was already sending steamers to Vera Cruz, to
bring back his homesick soldiers. Monarchy
will then be at an end in North America."
Maximilian's wife was in France, expecting
soon to see her husband. In a few weeks, the
corpse of the bandit-emperor, sustained by
French bayonets and shot by Mexican repub-

licans, and an insane widow startled Carleton, as it startled the world.

The *Journal* correspondent passed over to Napoleon's realm, spending a few weeks in Paris, Dijon, and other French cities. In Switzerland he enjoyed mightily the home of Calvin and its eloquent memories, Mont Blanc and its associated splendors, the mountains, the glaciers, the passes, and valleys, and, above all, his study of the politics of " The freest people of Europe." How truly prophetic was Carleton, when he wrote, " This republic, instead of being wiped off from the map, . . . will more likely become a teacher to Europe," — a truth never so large as now. He rode over the Splügen pass, and saw Milan and Verona. From the city of Romeo and Juliet, he took a carriage in order to visit and study, with the eye of an experienced engineer and veteran, the details of the battle of Custozza, where, on June 24th, 1866, the Archduke Albert gained the victory over the Italian La Marmora.

He reached Venice October 13th. In the old city proudly called the Queen of the Adriatic, and for centuries a republic, until ground under the heel of Austrian despotism, Carleton arrived in time to see the people almost insane with joy. The Austrian garrison was marching out and the Italian troops were moving in. The red caps and shirts of the Garibaldians brightened the throng in the streets, and the old stones of Venice, bathed in salt water at their bases, were deluged with bunting, flags, and rainbow colors. When King Victor Emmanuel entered, the scenes of joy and gladness, the sounds of music, the gliding gondolas, the illuminated marble palaces and humble homes, the worshipping hosts of people in the churches, and the singing bands in the streets, taxed to the utmost even Carleton's descriptive powers. The burden of joy everywhere was " Italy is one from the Alps to the Adriatic, and Venice is free."

Turning his attention to Rome, where French bayonets were still supporting the Pope's temporal throne, Carleton discussed a question of world-wide interest, — the impending loss of papal power and its probable results. Within a fortnight after his letter on this subject, the last echoes of the French drum-beat and bugle-blast had died away.

The red trousers of the Emperor's servants were numbered among Rome's mighty list of things vanished. In the Eternal City itself, Carleton attended mass at St. Peter's, and then reread and retold the story of both the Roman and the Holy Roman Empire. Some of his happiest days were passed in the studios of American artists and sculptors. There he saw, in their beginning of outlines and color, on canvas or in clay, some of the triumphs of art which now adorn American homes and cities. Fascinated as he was in Pompeii and in Rome with the relics and revelations of ancient life, he was even more thrilled by the rapid strokes of destiny in the modern world. The separation of church and state was being accomplished while Italy was waking to new life. The Anabaptists were avenged and justified.

About the middle of February, Carleton was again in Paris, seeing the Exposition and the Emperor of the French and his family. Then crossing to England, he heard a great debate over the Reform measures, in which Disraeli, Lowe, Bright, and Gladstone spoke. The results were the humiliation of Disraeli, and the break-up of the British ministry. Recrossing the channel to Paris, he spent eight weeks studying the Exposition and the country, writing many letters to the *Journal*. After examination of the great fortresses in the Duchy of Luxembourg, he went into Germany, tarrying at Heidelberg, Nuremberg, Munich, and Vienna. He then passed down "the beautiful blue Danube" to Buda-Pesth, where, having been given letters and commendations from J. L. Motley, the historian of the Netherlands and our minister at Vienna, he saw the glittering pageant which united the crowns of Austria and Hungary. This was performed in the parish church in Buda, an edifice built over six hundred years ago. It had been captured by the Turks and made into a mosque, where the muezzin supplanted the priest in calls of prayer. After the great victory won by John Sobieski, cross and altar were restored. Here, amid all the glittering and bewildering splendor of tapestry, banners, dynastic colors, national flags, jewels, and innumerable heraldic devices, "the iron crown of Charlemagne," granted by Pope Sylvester II. in the year 1000, and called "the holy and apostolic crown," was placed by Count Andrassy upon the head of the Emperor Francis Joseph. The ruler of Austria practically acknowledged the righteousness of the revolution of 1849, and his own mistake, when he accepted the crown from the once rebel militia-leader and then exiled Andrassy, having already given to the Hungarians the popular rights which they clamored for. Most gracious act of all, Francis Joseph contributed, with the Empress (whom Mrs. Coffin thought the handsomest woman in Europe), 100,000 ducats ($200,000) to the widows and children of those who were killed in 1849, while fighting against the empire. At this writing, December, 1896, we read of the unveiling, at Kormorn, of a monument to Klapka, the insurgent general of 1849.

In Berlin, Carleton saw a magnificent spectacle,— the review of the Prussian army in welcome to the Czar. He studied the battle-fields of Leipsig and Lutzen, and the ever continuing gamblers' war at Weisbaden. Then sailing down the Rhine, he revisited Paris to see the distribution of prizes at the Exposition, the array of Mohammedan and Christian princes, and the grand review of the French troops in honor of the Sultan. In England once more, he looked upon the great naval review of the British fleets of iron and wood. He studied the ritualistic movement. He attended the meeting of anti-ritualists at Salisbury, where, midway between matchless spire and preancient Cromlech, one can meditate on the evolution of religion. He was at the Methodist Conference of Great Britain in the city of Bristol, whence sailed the Cabots for the discovery of America, now four centuries ago. He read the modern lamentations of Thomas Carlyle, who, in his article, "Shooting the Niagara and After," foretold the death of good government and religion in the triumph of democracy.

At the British Scientific Association's gathering in Dundee, he heard Murchison, Baker, Lyell, Thomson, Tyndall, Lubbock, Rankine, Fairbairn, and young Professor Herschell. He was at the Social Science Congress held in Belfast, meeting Lord Dufferin, Dr. James McCosh, Goldwin Smith, and others. Two months more were given to study and observation in the countries Ireland, England

and Scotland, Holland and Belgium. Of his frequent letters to the *Journal* a score or so were written especially to and for young people, though all of them interested every class of readers. He kept a keen watch upon movements in Italy and in Spain, where the Carlists' uprising had begun.

In this manner, nearly sixteen months slipped away in parts of Europe, and amid scenes so remote as to require hasty journeys and much travelling. Carleton received further directions to continue his journey around the world. He was to visit the Holy Land, Egypt, India, China, and Japan, to cross the Pacific, and to traverse the United States as far as possible on the Pacific railway, then in course of construction. This was indeed "A New Voyage Around the World," not exactly in the sense of Defoe; but was, as Carleton called it in the book describing it, which he afterwards wrote, "Our New Way Around the World." No one before his time, so far as known, had gone around the globe, starting eastward from America, crossing continents, and using steam as the motor of transportation on land and water all the way.

Making choice of three routes to the Orient, Carleton left Paris December 9th, 1867, for Marseilles. He found much of the country thitherward nearly as forbidding as the hardest regions of New Hampshire. The climate was indeed easier than in the Granite State, but from November to March the people suffered more from cold than the Yankees. They lived in stone houses and fuel was dear. At Marseilles the vessels were packed so closely in docks, that the masts and spars reminded him of the slopes of the White Mountains after fire had swept the foliage away. Although innumerable tons of grain were imported here, he saw no elevators or labor saving appliances like those at Buffalo, which can load or empty ships' holds in a few half hours. Many of the imports were labelled "Service Militaire," and were for the support of that army of eight hundred thousand men, which the impoverished French people, even with a decreasing population, were so heavily taxed to support. Carleton noticed that merchants of France were planning to lay their hands on the East and win its trade.

CHAPTER XVIII

IT was "blowing great guns," and the sea was white with foam, when on the ninety-eighth anniversary of Washington's birthday into another world, December 14th, 1867, the steamer *Euphrates*, of the M. I. Company, left Marseilles. The iron ship was staunch, though not overclean. On the deck were boxed up eight carriages for Turks who had been visiting Paris. The captain amused himself, in hours which ought not to have been those of leisure, with embroidery. After a run through the Sardinian straits, they had clear sea room to Sicily. Stromboli was quiet, but Vesuvius was lively. At Messina they took on coal, oranges, five Americans, and one Englishman. On learning Carleton's plan to travel eastward to San Francisco, the Queen's subject remarked, with surprise:

"There was a time when we Englishmen had the routes of travel pretty much all to ourselves, but I'll be hanged if you Americans haven't crowded us completely off the sidewalk. We can't tie your shoe-strings."

Greece was sighted at sunrise. With Carleton's mental picture of the great naval victory of Navarino, by which the murderous Turk was driven off the sea, rose boyhood's remembrances of the fashionable "Navarino bonnets," with their colossal flaring fronts, with beds of artificial flowers set between brims and cheeks, making rivalry of color amid vast ostentation of bows and ribbon. With his glass, he could discern, at one point upon the hillside, the hut of a hermit, who had discovered that man cannot live upon history alone, but that beans and potatoes are desirable. The practical hermit cultivated a garden.

Arrival at Piræus was at 2 A. M. The party of passengers descended the ladder into a boat, and there sat shivering in their shawls, where they were likely to be left to historic meditation until the custom-house opened, except for the well-known fact that silver often conquers steel. One franc, held up before the gaze of a highly important personage possessed of a sword and much atmosphere of authority, secured smiles and welcome to the sacred soil of Greece, immunity from search, and direction to a café where all was warm and comfortable, and from which, in due time, hotel accommodations were secured.

In the city of Pericles, they saw the play of "Antigone" in the theatre of Herod Atticus. On visiting the Parthenon, with its marvellous sculpture, which Turkish soldiers had so often used as a target, they found that the chief inhabitants of the ruin were crows. They met the missionaries who were influential in the making of the new Grecian nation. From Athens they went to Constantinople, where Dr. Cyrus Hamlin, in Robert College, was lighting the beacon of hope for the Christians in the Turkish empire.

Leaving Europe at that end of it on which the Turks have encamped during four centuries, and where they are still blasting and devouring, Carleton visited Africa, the old house of bondage. At Alexandria his first greeting was a cry for bakshish. Within half an hour after landing, most of his childhood's illusions were dispelled. A drenching rain fell. The delta of the Nile had been turned into one vast cotton field which looked like a mass of snow. The clover was in bloom along the railway to Cairo. In this land of the donkey and of the Arabian Nights Entertainments, he received several practical lessons in the art of comparative swindling, soon learning that in roguery both Christians and the followers of the prophet are one.

In studying his Bible amid the lands which are its best commentary, Carleton concluded that the crossing of the Red Sea by the fugitive slaves from Egypt, over an " underground railway made by the order of God himself," " instead of being in the domain of the miraculous, is under natural law." At Suez, one of the half-way houses of the world, he was amused at the jollity of the Mohammedans, who had just broken their long lenten fast from tobacco and smoke, and who were very happy in their own way.

In thirty hours after leaving Alexandria, the party, now joined by Rev. E. B. Webb, had its first view of Palestine, — a sandy shore, low, level as a Western prairie, tufted with palms, green with olives, golden with orange orchards, and away in the distance an outline of gray mountains. Soon, in Jerusalem, he was among the donkeys, dogs, pilgrims, and muleteers. Out on the Mount of Olives and in starlit Bethlehem, by ancient Hebron, and then down to low-lying Jericho and at the Dead Sea, he was refreshing memory and imagination, shedding old fancies and traditions, discriminating as never before between figures of rhetoric and figures of rock and reality, while feeding his faith and cheering his spirit. Then from Jerusalem, after a twenty days' stay, the party rode northward to Shechem, the home of the Samaritan, and over the plain of Esdraelon. There Carleton's military eye revelled in the scene, and he made mind-pictures of the battles fought there during all the centuries. Then, after tarrying at Nazareth and Beyrout, we find him, April 11th, at Suez, on board a steamer for the East.

At Paris he had seen De Lesseps, amid tumultuous applause, receive from Napoleon III. a gold medal.

Now Carleton was on the steamship *Baroda*, moving down the Red Sea, once thought to be an arm of the Indian Ocean, but which we now know to be only a portion of "the great rift valley," — the longest and deepest and widest trough on the earth's surface, which extends from the base of Mount Lebanon and the Sea of Galilee, through the Jordan Valley, the Dead Sea, the dried up wadies, the Red Sea, and the chain of lakes and Nyanzas discovered in recent years in the heart of Africa, and extending nearly to Zanzibar. Passing by Great Britain's garrisons, lighthouses, and coaling stations, which guard her pathway to India, Bombay was reached April 27th.

In the interior, in the distressing hot weather of India, Carleton found this the land of punkas, tatties, and odors both sweet and otherwise. He was impressed with the amount of jewelry seen, not in the bazaars, but on the persons of the women. "Through all ages India has swallowed up silver, and the absorption is as great as ever to-day." He was amused at the little men's big heads, covered with a hundred and fifty feet, or more, of turban material, which made so many of them look like exaggerated tulips. He noticed the phenomena of religion, the trees smeared with paint, the Buddhist caves, the Parsee Towers of Silence, the phallic emblems of nature-worship. Evidently he was not converted to cremation, for he wrote, " The earth is our mother, and it is sweeter to lie on her bosom amid blooming flowers or beneath bending elms and sighing pines in God's Acre." He noticed how rapidly the railways were breaking down caste. "The locomotive, like a ploughshare turning the sward of the prairies, is cutting up a faith whose roots run down deep into bygone ages. . . . The engine does not turn out for obstructions, such as in former days impeded the car of progress."

Though caste was stronger than the instincts of humanity, this relic of the brutishness of conquest was not allowed to have sway in railway carriages.

Carleton sums up his impressions of the religions of India in this sentence : " The world by wisdom knew not God." He found his preconceived ideas of central India all wrong. Instead of jungles, were plateaus, forest-covered mountains, groves, and bamboo. With the thermometer at 105° in the shade, the woodwork shrunk so that the drivers of the dak or ox-cart wound the spokes of the wheels with straw and kept them wet, so that Carleton noticed them "watering their carriage as well as horses." Whether it was his head that swelled or his hat which shrunk, he found the latter two sizes too small at night. In India, between June and October, little business is done. The demand for cotton, caused by the American war, had set India farmers to growing the bolls over vast areas, but the cost of carriage to the seaboard was so great that new roads had to be built.

"Sahib Coffin" at the garrison towns was amused at both the young British officers, with their airs, and at the old veterans, who were as dignified as mastiffs. Living in the central land of the world's fairy tales, he enjoyed these legends which "give perfume to literature, science, and art." At Allahabad, in the middle of the fort, he saw a pillar forty-two feet high, erected by King Asoka, 250 B. C., bearing an inscription commanding kindness to animals. In one part of India, at the golden pagoda of Benares, he found the monkeys worshipped as gods, or at least honored as divine servants, while in the North they were pests and thieves, the enemy of the farmer.

Among other hospitalities enjoyed, was a dinner with an American, Mr. C. L. Brown, who represented the Tudor Ice Company, of Boston, and who sold solidified water from Wenham Lake. The piece that clinked in the glass of Carleton, "sparkling and bright in its liquid light," had been harvested in 1865, three years before. He described it as a "piece of imprisoned cold, fragment of a bygone winter," which called up "bright pictures of boys and girls with their rosy cheeks and flashing skates, — a breeze of old associations." At Benares, various root ideas of Hindoo holiness were illustrated, including the linga worship and the passion for motherhood in that strange phallic cult which, from India to Japan, has survived all later forms of religion. In Calcutta, Old India had already been forgotten in the newer and more Christian India. He visited especially the American Union Mission Home, where Miss Louise Hook and Miss Britton were training the girls of India to nobler ideals and possibilities of life. After seeing the school, Carleton wrote : " Theirs is a great work. Educate the women of India, and we withdraw two hundred millions from gross idolatry. This mighty moral leverage obtained, the whole substratum of society will be raised to a higher level. The mothers of America fought the late war through to its glorious end. They sustained the army by their labor, their sympathy, their heroic devotion. The mothers of India are keeping the idols on their pedestals."

Personal accidents in India were minor and amusing, mostly. Crossing the Bay of Bengal on the *Clan Alpine*, one of England's opium steamers bound to China, a boiler blew up. The "priming" of the iron, the life of the metal, having been burned out in passing from fresh to salt water, was the cause of the trouble. Nineteen persons, eighteen natives and a Scotsman, were killed or badly scalded. Carleton rushed out from his stateroom, amid clouds of steam that made his path nearly invisible, and was happy in finding his wife safe on deck at the stern. At sunset the Christian was given the rites of burial. The dead Hindoos, not being used to religious attentions paid to corpses, were heaved into the sea, and the voyage continued. This was not the first or the last time that Carleton experienced the sensation of being blown up while on a steamboat.

CHAPTER XIX

A T Penang, in the Spice Islands, the verge of the Flowery Kingdom seemed to have been reached. "We might say that that land had bloomed over its own borders, and its blossoms had fallen here. . . . Nearly the entire population of this island, 125,000 in all, are Chinese." At Singapore, the town of lions, he met an American hunter named Carroll, who lived with the natives and had won fame as a dead shot. Fortunately for humanity, that contests with the aboriginal beasts a possession of this part of the earth, the leonine fathers frequently devour their cubs, else the earth would be overrun with the lions.

Seventeen days on the *Clan Alpine* passed by, and then, on the 10th of June, the captain pointed out the "Asses' Ears," two black specks on the distant horizon, which gave them their first glimpse of China.   On Saturday afternoon, Mrs. Coffin had the pleasure of being told, by the healthy-looking captain of the sampan or boat by which they were to get ashore, that she was "a red-faced foreign devil."   This was a Chinese woman, of thirty-five or forty, who commanded the craft.   The next day, Sunday, they went to church in sedan-chairs, and sat under the punkas or swinging-fans, which cooled the air.   On Monday, while going around with, or calling upon, the missionaries Preston, Kerr, and Parker, the Americans who had a sense of the value of minutes found that the " Chinese are an old people.   Their empire is finished, their civilization complete, and time is a drug."   The walls of the great Roman Catholic Cathedral, costing over four million dollars, were then but half-way up.

Being a true Christian, without cant or guile, Carleton, as a matter of course, was a warm friend of the missionaries, and always sought them out to visit and cheer them.   He rarely became their guest, or accepted hospitality under the roofs either of American consuls or missionaries, lest critics might say his views were colored by the glasses of others.   He would have his own mind and opinions judicial. Nevertheless, he knew that those who knew the language of the people were good guides and helpers to intelligent impressions. In Shanghai he met Messrs. Yates, Wilson, and Thomson, and, in the Sailors' Chapel, Rev. E. W. Syle, afterwards president of the Asiatic Society of Japan. Carleton noticed that when the collection was taken up among the tars present, the plate, when returned, showed several silver dollars. The travellers went up the Yangtse in a New York built Hudson River steamer, commanded by a Yankee captain from Cape Ann. At Wuchang he called on Bishop Williams, whom he had met in London at the Pan-Anglican council, and who afterwards made so noble record of work in the Mikado's empire.

So far from being appalled at what he saw of the Chinese and their civilization, Carleton noted many things to admire,—their democratic spirit, their competitive civil service examinations, and their reverence for age and parental authority. At the dinners occasionally eaten in a Chinese restaurant, he asked no questions as to whether the animal that furnished the meat barked, mewed, bellowed, or whinnied, but took the mess in all good conscience.

From the middle of the Sunrise Kingdom, the passage was made on the American Pacific mail-steamer *Costa Rica*, through a great storm. In those days before lighthouses, the harbor of Nagasaki was reached through a narrow inlet, which captains of ships were sometimes puzzled to find. They steamed under and within easy range of the fifty or more bronze cannon, mounted on platforms under sheds along the cliffs. Except at Shimonoséki, in 1863 and 1864, when floating and fast fortresses, steamers and land-batteries exchanged their shots, to the worsting of the Choshiu clansmen, the military powers of the Japanese had not yet been tested. Accepting the local traditions about the Papists' Hill, or Papenberg, from which, in 1637, the insurgent Christians are said to have been hurled into the sea, Carleton wrote, " The gray cliff, wearing its emerald crown, is an everlasting memorial to the martyr dead."

It was in this harbor that the American commander, James Glynn, in 1849, in the little fourteen-gun brig *Preble*, gave the imperious and cruel Japanese of Tycoon times a taste of the lesson they were to learn from McDougall and Pearson. Soon they reached Déshima, the little island which, in Japan's modern history, might well be called its leaven; for here, for over two centuries, the Dutch dispensed those ideas, as well as their books and merchandise, which helped to make the Japan of our day. Carleton's impressions of the Japanese were that they had a more manly physique, and were less mildly tempered, but that they were lower in morals, than the Chinese. The women were especially eager to know the mysteries of crinoline, and anxiously inspected the dress of their foreign sisters.

Japan, in 1868, was in the throes of civil war. The lamp of history at that time was set in a dark lantern, and very few of the foreigners, diplomatic, missionary, or mercantile, then in the islands, had any clear idea of what was going on, or why things were moving as they were. It may be safely said that only a handful of students, who had made themselves familiar with the ancient native records, and with that remarkable body of native literature produced in the first half of this century, could see clearly through the maze, and explain the origin and meaning of the movement of the great southern clans and daimios against the Tycoon. It was in reality the assertion of the Mikado's imperial and historic claims to complete supremacy against the Shogun's or lieutenant's long usurpation. It was an expression of nationality against sections. The civil war meant "unite or die." Carleton naturally shared in the general wrong impressions and darkness that prevailed, and neither his letters nor his writing give much light upon the political problem, though his descriptions of the scenery and of the people and their ways make pleasing reading. In reality, even as the first gun against Sumter and the resulting civil war were the results of the clash of antagonistic principles which had been working for centuries, so the uprising and war in Japan in 1868–70, which resulted in national unity, one government, one ruler, one flag, the overthrow of feudalism, the abolition of ancient abuses, and the making of new Japan, resulted from agencies set in motion over a century before. Foreign intercourse and the presence of aliens on the soil gave the occasion, but not the cause, of the nation's re-birth.

The new government already in power at Kioto, under pressure of bigoted Shintoists, revamped the ancient cult of Shinto, making it a political engine. Persecution of the native Christians, who had lived, with their faith uneradicated, on the old soil crimsoned by the blood of their martyr ancestors, had already begun. Carleton found on the steamer going North to Nagasaki one of the French missionaries in Japan, who informed him that at least twenty thousand native Christians were in communication with their spiritual advisers. At sea they met the Japanese steamer named after Sir Harry Parkes, the able and energetic British minister, who was one of the first to understand the situation and to recognize the Mikado. This steamer had left Nagasaki three weeks previously, with four hundred native Christians. These had been tied, bundled, and numbered like so many sticks of firewood, and carried northward to the mountain-crater prisons of Kaga.

Many of these prisoners I afterwards saw. When in Boston I used to talk with Mr. Coffin about Japanese history and politics, and of the honored Guido F. Verbeck, one of the finest of scholars, noblest of missionaries, and best friends of Japan. No one was more amused than Carleton over that mistake, in his letter and book, from hearsay, about " Mr. Verbeck, a Dutchman who is trading there " (Nagasaki).

They passed safely through the straits of Shimonoséki, admiring the caves, the surf, the multitudes of sea-fowl, the silver streams falling down from the heights of Kokura, on the opposite side of Choshiu, and from mountains four thousand feet high, and made beautiful with terraces and shrubbery. Through the narrow strait where the water ran like a mill-race, the steamer ploughed her way. They passed heights not then, as a few years before, dotted numerously with the black muzzles of protruding cannon, nor fortified as they are now with steel domes, heavy masonry, and modern artillery. Here in this strait, in 1863, the gallant David McDougall, in the U. S. corvette *Wyoming*, performed what was perhaps the most gallant act ever wrought by a single commander in a single ship, in the annals of our navy. Here, in 1864, the United States, in alliance with three European Powers, went to war with one

Parrott gun under Lieutenant Pierson on the *Ta-Kiang*.

Like nearly all other first gazers upon the splendid panorama of the Inland Sea, Carleton was enthralled with the ever changing beauty, while interested in the busy marine life. At one time he counted five hundred white wings of the Old Japan's bird of commerce, the junk. At the new city of Hiogo, with the pretty little settlement of Kobé yet in embryo, they spent a happy day, having Dr. W. A. P. Martin to read for them the inscriptions in the Chinese characters on the Shinto temple stones and tablets.

The ship then moved northward, through that wonder river in the ocean, the Kuro-Shiwo, or Black Current, the Gulf Stream of the Pacific, first discovered and described by the American captain, Silas Bent. The great landmarks were clearly visible, — Idzu, with its mountains and port of Shimoda, where Townsend Harris had won the diplomatic victory which opened Japan to foreign residence and commerce; white-hooded Fuji San, looking as chaste and pure as a nun, with her first dress of summer snow; Vries Island, with its column

of gray smoke. Further to the east were the
Bonin Islands, first visited by Captain Reuben
Coffin, of Nantucket, in the ship *Transit*, in
1824. When past Saratoga Spit, Webster Isle,
and Mississippi Bay, the party stepped ashore
at Yokohama, where on the hill was a British
regiment in camp. The redcoats had been
ordered from India during the dangers consequent upon civil strife, and belonged to the
historic Tenth Regiment, which Carleton's
grandfather and his fellow patriots had met on
Bunker Hill.

It was a keen disappointment to Carleton
not to be able to see Tokio, then forbidden to
the tourist, because of war's commotion. A
heavy battle had been fought July 4, 1868, at
Uyéno, of old the place of temples, and now
of parks and exhibitions, in the northern part
of the city. The Mikado's forces then moved
on the strongholds of the rebels at Aidzu, but
foreigners knew very little of what was then
going on. After a visit to the mediæval capital of the Shoguns, at Kamakura, he took the
steamer southward to Nagasaki, and again set
his face eastward. He was again a traveller to
the Orient, that is, to America. On the home-

ward steamer, the *Colorado*, were forty-one first-class passengers, of whom sixteen were going to Europe, taking this new, as it was the nearest and cheapest, way home. Below deck were one thousand Chinese. Before the steamer got out of the harbor it stopped, at the request of Admiral Rowan, and four unhappy deserters were taken off.

The Pacific Ocean was crossed in calm. It seemed but a very few days of pleasant sailing on the great peaceful ocean, — with the days' gorgeous sunrises and sunsets, which hollowed out of the sky caverns upon caverns of light full of color more wonderful than Ali Baba's treasure-chamber, and nights spiritually lovely with the silvery light of moon and stars. On August 15th, 1868, they passed through the Golden Gate, and " Aladdin's palace of the West," the cosmopolitan city of San Francisco, was before their eyes.

Not more wonderful than the things ephemeral and the strange changes going on in the city, wherein were very few old men, but only the young and strong of many nations, were the stabilities of life. Carleton found time to examine and write about education, the libraries, churches, asylums, charities, and the beginnings of literature, science, and art.   In one of the schools he found them debating " whether Congress was right in ordering Major Andre to be executed."   Lest some might think Carleton lacking in love to " Our Old Home," we quote, "It is neither politic, wise, nor honest to instill into the youthful mind animosity towards England or any other nation, especially for acts committed nearly a century ago."

In his youth he had played the battles of Bunker Hill and Bennington, in which his living ancestors had fought, and of which they had told him, — using the roadside weeds as British soldiers, and sticks, stones, and a cornstalk knife for weapons.   In after-life, he often expressed the emphatic opinion that our school histories were viciously planned and written, preserving a spirit that boded no good for the future of our country and the world.   In the nineties, he was asked by the Harpers to write a history of the United States for young people.   This he hoped to do, correcting prejudices, and emphasizing the moral union between the two nations using English speech ;

but all too soon the night came when he could not do the work proposed.

Remaining in California over two months, Carleton started eastward in the late autumn over the Central Pacific railway, writing from Salt Lake City what he saw and knew about Mormonism and the polygamy and concubinage there shamefully prevalent. From the town of Argenti, leaving the iron rails, they enjoyed and suffered seven days and nights of staging until smooth iron was entered upon once more. They passed several specimens of what Carleton called "pandemonium on wheels," — those temporary settlements swarming with gamblers and the worst sort of human beings, male and female. They abode some time in the city of Latter Day Saints. They saw Chicago. "Home Again" was sung before Christmas day. Once more he breathed the salt air of Boston. Carleton wrote a series of letters on "The Science of Travel," showing where, when, and for how much, one could enjoy himself in the various countries and climates in going around the world.

Carleton summed up his impressions after completing the circuit of the globe in declaring that three aggressive nations, England, Russia, and the United States, were the chief makers of modern history,—America being the greatest teacher of them all, and "our flag the symbol of the world's best hope."

CHAPTER XX

THE GREAT NORTHWEST

IT was one of the great disappointments of Carleton's life that, on returning from his journey around the world, he was not made, as he had with good reason fully expected to be made, chief editor of the *Boston Journal*. We need not go into details of the matter, but suffice it to say, that Carleton was not one to waste time in idle regrets. Indeed, his was a character that could be tested by disappointments, which, in his life, were not a few. Instead of bitterness, came the ripened fruit of patience and mellowness of character.

His renewed acquaintance with the region west of the Mississippi, which he had made during his recent trip across the continent, only whetted his appetite for more seeing and knowing of the future seat of America empire. He accepted with pleasure a commission to explore the promising regions of Minnesota and Dakota, and to give an account especially of the Red River Valley.

Already, in 1858, he had written and published, at his own expense, a pamphlet of twenty-three pages, entitled "The Great Commercial Prize," Boston, A. Williams & Co. It cost him fifty dollars, then a large sum for him, from which the advantage accrued to the nation at large. It was addressed to every American who values the prosperity of his country. It was "An inquiry into the present and prospective commercial position of the United States, and a plea for the immediate construction of a railroad from Missouri River to Puget Sound." It opens with a review of the great events in the world which have had a direct and all-important bearing upon the United States. Hitherto, since the modern mastery of the ocean through the mariner's compass and the science of navigation, the Atlantic had been the domain of sea power. The Pacific was in future to be the scene of greater opportunities and grander commercial developments. With China and Japan entering the brotherhood of nations, and Russia extending its power towards the Pacific, " five hundred millions of human beings were henceforth to be reached by the hand of civilization." The countries and continents bordering the greatest of oceans were animated with new ideas of progress. On our own western shores, California, Oregon, and Washington were awaiting the touch of industry to yield their riches.

As a reader of the signs of the times, Carleton pointed out the great changes which were to take place in the thoroughfares of trade and travel. Instead of civilization depending for its communication with India, China, and Japan, by passages around the southern capes of the two continents, the paths of water and land traffic were to be directly from China, Russia, and Japan to northern America. Noticing that England had made herself the world's banking-house, he saw that the time had come when the United States (which he believed to be potentially, at least, a larger and a nobler England) must stretch out her left hand, as well as her right, for the grasping of the world's prizes. He pointed out the wonderful openings along the shore, providing harbors at the mouths of the two great river systems

on the Pacific Coast, those of the Sacramento
and the Columbia.

Carleton urged that " A railroad to Puget
Sound, constructed immediately, alone will
take the key of the Northwest from the hands
of the nations which stand with us in the front
rank of power. "   Important as the railway to
San Francisco was, it would not yield the
prize.   To his vision it was even then perfectly clear, as to all the world it has been since
the Chino-Japanese war of 1894–95, that the
chief American staple which China and Japan
needs is cotton, though machinery, petroleum,
and flour are in demand.   After giving facts,
statistics, and well-wrought arguments, he
wrote : " Again we say it is easy for America to
lay its hand upon the greatest prize of all
times, to make herself the world's workshop,—
the world's banker.   Shall England or the
United States control the northwestern section
of the continent and the trade of the Pacific ? "

Over a decade later on, in 1869, Carleton
revelled in the opportunity of being once more
the herald and informer concerning regions
ready to welcome the plough, the machine-shop,
the home, the church, the school, and the glo-

ries of civilization. He spent several months mostly in the open air and chiefly on horseback, though often on foot and in vehicles of various descriptions, camping out under the stars, or accepting such rough accommodation as was then afforded in regions where palace cars, elegant hotels, and comfortable homes are now commonplaces. His letters to the *Journal* were breezy and sparkling. They diffused the aroma of the Western forests and prairies, while marked with that same wealth of graphic detail, spice of anecdote, lambent humor, and garnish of a conversation which delighted the readers of his correspondence from the army and from the older seats of empire in Asia and in Europe. Carleton's literary photographs were the means of moving many a young and adventurous couple from their homes in the East to the frontier, and of firing the ambition of many a lad and lass to seek their fortune west of the Mississippi. Since California was settled and the Pacific Coast occupied even at scattered points, our frontiers, strange as it may seem, have not been at the eastern or western ends, but on the middle of the country.

After this campaign of correspondence, Carleton returned home and wrote that little book which has been so widely read, both in the East and in the West, entitled " The Seat of Empire." It was published in 1870 by Fields & Co., of Boston. It had eight pages of introduction, with a map of the territory yet to be settled. It was a volume of 232 pages, 16mo, and was illustrated. For many years afterwards, amid the hundreds of letters received from grateful readers of his books, none seemed to give Carleton more pleasure than those from readers who had become settlers. This little book had indeed come to many as a revelation of the promised land. The contagion reached even to Mrs. Coffin's brothers, one of whom, with a nephew of Carleton, became a pioneer farmer in the Red River Valley in Dakota.

Another pathfinder, a literary as well as military pioneer in opening this noble region to civilization, was the warm friend of Carleton and of the writer, General Henry B. Carrington, of the United States regular army, and author of that standard authority, " Battles of the American Revolution." During the Civil

War, General Carrington had been stationed in Indiana, where he was the potent agent in spoiling the treasonable schemes of the Knights of the Golden Circle, and in nobly seconding Governor Morton in holding the State true to the Union. The war over, he served on the Western plains until 1868, and then wrote "Absaraka, the Home of the Crows," which was a score of years afterwards republished under the title of " Absaraka, the Land of Massacre." General Carrington was afterwards one of the active members of Shawmut Church. With his fine scholarly and literary tastes, he made a delightful companion.

Any well-told narrative of the exploration, conquest, and civilization of a country, with a history which has helped to make the pageant and procession of human achievement so rich, is, when fully known, of thrilling interest. How grand is the story of the Aryans in India, of the first historic invaders of Japan, of the Roman advance into northern Europe, of the making of Africa and of western America in our own times! Even the culture-epoch of the North American Indians, as written by

Longfellow, in his "Song of Hiawatha," is as fascinating as a fairy tale.

Carleton, believing himself and his country to be " in the foremost files of time " and " the heirs of all the ages," came, saw, and wrote of our empire in the Northwest, with an intoxication of delight. Furthermore, he believed that those who came after him would see vastly more of this part of the earth replenished and subdued. Yet the conquest for which he longed was not to be with blood. His hope and his purpose were intensely ethical and spiritual. His vision was of the triumph of peace, law, order, religion. He urged emigrants looking beyond the Mississippi, or the Rockies, to go in groups, and take with them " the moral atmosphere of their old homes." He advocated the opening of a school the first week and a Sunday school the first Sunday following the arrival of such a colony at its destination. Even a bare, new home, cramped and poor, he suggested, might be to them the type of a better one in more prosperous years, and of the Home beyond, so that, from the beginning, " on Sabbath morning, swelling upward on the air, sweeter than the lay of the lark among the flowers, will ascend the songs of the Sunday school established in their new home. Looking forward with ardent hope of the earthly prosperous years, they would look still beyond to the heavenly, and sing:

> ' My heavenly home is bright and fair;
>   Nor pain nor death can enter there.' "

In Japan's long and brilliant roll of benefactors and civilizers, no names shine more gloriously than those of the Openers of Mountain paths, — of men, priests or laymen, who, by showing the way, surmounting the dangers and difficulties, revealed and made accessible great spaces of land for home and harvest field. The Hebrew prophet speaks eloquently of those who " raise up the foundation of many generations," and of those called "the restorer of the paths to dwell in." In this glorious company of the world's benefactors, Carleton's name is written indelibly. Even " far-sighted" men deemed the project of a railway to Puget Sound " visionary," when Carleton's pamphlet was published. He lived to see it a reality.

CHAPTER XXI

THE WRITER OF HISTORY

STEEPED in the ancestral lore of New England, a student of the origins of this country, a reader of, and thinker upon, the records of the past, having seen history in its making, and, as it were, in the very furnace and crucibles of war, having traversed the globe along the line of its highest civilizations, having watched at the cradle of our own nobler empire in the great West, Carleton determined to write for the young people of this nation the story of liberty, and of liberty's highest expression, " The American People and Their Government."

It was not a sudden impulse that came to him, it was no accident, but the result of a deliberate purpose.   Opportunity and leisure now made the way perfectly clear.   He had long been of the opinion that the events of history might be presented vividly to the youthful mind in a series of pictures. He would portray the experiences of individuals whom the reader has been led to regard as persons, and not merely parts of an army, a church, and a government. He believed this was a better method, with young readers at least, than that usually followed by the majority of writers of history. To form his style, he read and re-read the very best English authors. He studied Burke especially, and ascribed to him the strongest single literary influence he had known. Years afterwards, when (like the swords of the Japanese steel-smiths, Muramasa and Sanémori, which never would rest quietly in their scabbards, but always kept flying out) Carleton's books were nearly always usefully absent from the shelves, the librarian at Dover, New Hampshire, in surprise made criticism to his face of Carleton's own statement about Burke. She remarked to him that she had not thought of Burke as a model for a person intending to write fiction, — referring, doubtless, to " Winning His Way," and " Caleb Krinkle."

Carleton replied that the strong, fine style of the British author gave him the best possible lesson in presenting a subject. "Whether writing fiction or fact, if the author wished to make and retain an impression on the mind of his reader, let him study Burke." At a particular time, as the chief librarian of a large public library told him, Carleton's books were more largely read than those of any living writer in the world.

"Caleb Krinkle" is a story of American life in which the characters, the habits of thought, and the rich details of daily routine are given with minuteness, accuracy of observation, and genuine sympathy. The landscape is that of New Hampshire, but the outlook is far beyond, for the author's purpose is to sow broadcast the seeds of true dignity, manliness, and republicanism. The hero is a good one, but of no uncommon type.

The young Yankee finds the battle of life hard, but also fights it bravely, and, in good time, conquers. The secondary actor, Dan Dishaway, is a wholly original character, a tin peddler with little education and unpolished manners, but with a loyal heart, and a simple, unconscious character that impressed and influenced the whole village. The teacher of teachers, to him, was his mother. The very foundation of the story is the value of human character, apart from the accidents of birth or position. The plot develops rapidly, and is illustrated by exciting incidents of river freshets, shipwreck on one of the great lakes, and a prairie fire. Love is shown to be no respecter of persons, but is found faithful, pure, and delicate, in people who never heard of cosmic philosophy, or the term "altruism," who knew not the classics, who went sadly astray in grammar. Without direct preaching, the story shows that the way of the transgressor is hard, and that the hardness is not lessened by worldly prosperity.

The critic quickly notices, however, that Carleton is not so successful in his pictures of city life as those of the country. Nevertheless, in modern days, when the population of Boston consists not of people born there, but chiefly of newcomers from the country, from Canada, or from Europe, Carleton was all the more a helper. An American who has mastered French, even though not perfect in pronunciation, may be a better teacher of it than a native.

Bertha Wayland's success in society, and her Boston life, made a very attractive portion of the book to a large number of readers at rural firesides.   For who in New England, and still young, does not hope some day to live in sight of the golden dome?   In later years, " Caleb Krinkle " was republished, with some revision and in much handsomer form, as " Dan of Mill-brook," by Estes and Lauriat, of Boston.

His next work, which still remains the most popular of all, the one least likely to suffer by the lapse of time, and the last probably to reach oblivion, because it appeals to young Americans in the whole nation, is his " Boys of '76."   The first lore to which Carleton listened after his infant lips had learned prayer, and " line upon line, and precept upon precept," from the Bible, was from his soldier-grand-fathers.   These around the open fireplace told the story of Revolutionary marches, and camps, and battles.   Nothing could be more real to the open-eyed little boy than the narratives related by the actors themselves, especially when he could ask questions, and get full light and explanation.

For an author who would write on the beginnings of the Revolution, no part of our country is so rich in historic sites, and so superbly equipped with libraries, museums, relics, and memorials, as the valley of the Charles River, in Massachusetts. In this region lies Boston, where not the first, though nearly the first, blood of the Revolution was shed; where were hung for Paul Revere the lantern-beacons; which was first the base of operations against Bunker Hill; and which afterward suffered siege, and served as the outlet for the Tories to Canada, when Howe and his fleet sailed away. Across the river is the battle-road to Lexington, now nobly marked with monumental stones and tablets, and, further on, Lexington itself, with its blood-consecrated green and inscribed boulder, its museum, and its well-marked historic spots. Beyond is Concord, with its bridge, well-site, and bronze minuteman. From the crest of the green mound on Bunker Hill, at Charlestown, rises the granite monument seen from all the country round. Near to Boston, is Cambridge with its university, Washington's elm, and manifold Revolutionary memories; while on the southeast, on the rising ground close at hand, and now part of the municipality itself, are Dorchester Heights, once fortified and bristling with cannon. Within easy reach by rail, water, or wheel, are places already magnetic to the tourist and traveller, because their reputations have been richly enlarged by poet, artist, romancer, and historian. Along the coast, or slightly inland, stood the humble homes of the ancestors of Grant and Lincoln, and but a little further to the southeast is the "holy ground" of Plymouth.

Even more important to the historiographer are the amazing treasures of books and records gathered in the twin cities on the Charles, making a wealth of material for American history, unique in the United States. What wonder, then, that the overwhelming majority of American writers of history have wrought here? Nor need we be surprised that, both in their general tone and in the bulk of their writing, they have portrayed less the real history of the United States than the history of New England, — with a glance at parts adjacent and an occasional distant view of regions beyond.

Graphic, powerful, and popular as are Carleton's books, he does not wholly escape the limitations of his heredity and environment. Generous as he is, and means to be, to other States, nationalities, and sections in the United States, beyond those in the six Eastern States, the student more familiar with the great constructive forces of the Middle, the Southern, and the Western States, who knows the power of Princeton as well as of Harvard, of Dutch as well as of Yankee, without necessarily contesting Carleton's statements of fact, is inclined to discern larger streams of influence, and to give greater credit to sources and developments of power, and to men and institutions west and south of the Hudson River, than does Carleton in his books.

Yet to the millions of his readers, history seemed to be written in a new way. It was different from anything to which they had been accustomed. Peter Parley had, indeed, in his time, created a fresh style of historical narration, which captivated unnumbered readers by its simple and direct method of presenting subjects known in their general outline, but not made of sufficient human or present interest. These works had suited exactly the stage of culture which the majority of young people

in our country had reached when the Parley
books were written. It is doubtful, however,
whether those same works would have achieved
a like success in the last three decades of this
century. Education had been so much improved, schools were so much more general,
the development of the press and cheap reading matter was so great, that in the enlargement
of view consequent upon the successful issue
of the great civil war, a higher order of historical narration was a necessity. He who would
win the new generation needed to be neither
a professional scholar, a man of research, nor a
genius, but he must know human nature well,
and be familiar with great national movements,
the causes and the channels of power. This
equipment, together with a style fashioned,
indeed, in the newspaper office, but deepened
and enriched by the study of language, of
rhetoric, and of masterly literary methods, as
seen in the best English prose, made Carleton
the elect historian for the new generation, and
the educator of the youth of our own and the
coming century.

Carleton is a maker of pictures. He turns
types into prismatics, and paragraphs into paint-

ings. He lifts the past into the present. The event is seen as though it happened yesterday, and the persons, be they kings or plough-boys, appear as if living to-day. Their hearts, affections, motives, thoughts, are just like those of men and women in our time. Their clothing and way of living may be different, but they are the sort of human beings with which we are acquainted. Better yet, it is not only the men with crowns on their heads, or the women who wear jewelled and embroidered robes, or riders locked up in steel, or men under tonsure or tiara, that did great things and made the world move. Carleton shows how the milk-maid, the wagoner, the blacksmith, the spinster with the distaff, the rower of the boat, the common soldier on foot, the student in his cell, and the peddler with his pack, all had a part in working out the wonderful story.

Had a part, did I say? No, in Carleton's story he *has* a part. No writer more frequently and with keener effect uses the historical present. Compare Carleton's straightforward narration and marching chapters with the average British writer of history, and at once

we see the difference between chroniclers, —
who give such enormous space to kings, queens
and ecclesiastical and military figure-heads, almost to the extent (in the eye of the philosophic student, at least) of caricature, — and
this modern scribe, to whom every true man
is a sovereign, while a king is no more than a
man. While well able to measure personal-
ities and forces, to divine causes, and to discern and emphasize in the foreground of his
pictures, even as an artist does, the important
figure, yet Carleton is never at a loss to do this
because the real hero may be of humble birth
or in modest apparel.

In travelling, the little child from the car
window will notice many things in the landscape and about the houses passed, belonging
to his lowly world of experience, no higher
than the top of a yardstick, to which the
average adult is blind. Carleton looked with
the child's eye over history's field. He brings
before the front lights of his stage what will at
once catch the attention of the young people,
to whom the deeper things of life may be
invisible mystery. Yet, Carleton's books are
always enjoyable to the mature man, for he

discerns beneath the vivid picturing and simple rhetoric, so pleasing to the child, a practical knowledge and a philosophic depth which
shows that the writer is a master of the art of
reading men and events as well as of interpreting history.

Mr. Coffin's more serious productions are
his arguments before Congressional and State
legislative committees; his pamphlets on the
labor question, railways, and patents; his addresses before general audiences and gatherings
of scientific, commercial, and religiously interested men; his life of Garfield, as well as that
of Lincoln; and those voluminous contribu-
tions made to the daily or weekly press, and
to magazines, and to reviews. Editors often
turned to him for that kind of light and
knowledge that the public needed when grave
issues were before the church, the city, the
commonwealth, the nation. In speaking or
writing thus, he used a less ornate style, less
fervid rhetoric, and spoke or wrote with direct,
business-like precision. In a word, he suited
his style to the work in hand. But, because
he attracted and delighted, while teaching, his
young readers, that critic must be blind or un-

appreciative who cannot see also the purpose of a master mind. The mature intellect of Carleton which animates and informs the pretty stories, educated also up and on to the nobler heights of historical reading.

Strictly speaking, in the light of the more rigid canons of historical knowledge and the research demanded in our days, and when tested by stern criticism, Mr. Coffin was not a historical scholar of the first order. Nor did he make any such pretension. No one, certainly not himself, would dream of ranging his name in the same line with those of the great masters, Prescott, Motley, Bancroft, or Parkman, — men of wealth and leisure, as well as of ability. He painted his pictures without going into the chemistry of colors, or searching into the mysteries of botany, to be absolutely sure as to the classification of the fibres which made his canvas. His first purpose was to make an impression, and his second, to fix that impression inerasably on the mind. For this, he trusted largely the work of those who had lived before him, and he made diligent and liberal use of materials already accumulated. He would paint his own picture after making the drawings and arranging his tints, perspective, lights, and shadows.

Nevertheless, Mr. Coffin was not a man accustomed to take truth at second hand. His own judgment was singularly sane, and he was not accustomed to receive statements and to devour them unflavored by the salt of criticism. Four years of the pursuit of letters amid arms, while passion was hottest, and men were too excited to care for the exact truth, had trained this cool-headed scribe to critical treatment of rumors and reports. Furthermore, he knew the value of first authorities and of contemporary writers and eye-witnesses. He discounted much of the writing done after the war in controversy, for political ends, for personal vanity, or to cover up damaged reputations. He knew both the heating and the cooling processes of time. I remember when, about 1890, after he had finished making a set of scrap-books of soldiers' letters, reminiscences and newspaper reports of the battles of the war, how heartily he laughed when, with twinkling eyes, he remarked on the tendency of some old soldiers "to remember a good deal that never happened." As his experience with the pen deepened, he became more rigid in his requirements as to the quality of the information which his books gave. Those who have read especially his four later volumes on the war, will note that at the end of each chapter he gives the sources of authority for his statements and judgments. In a word, Carleton was a man who, having mapped the irrigated country and the stream's mouth, resolutely set his face towards the fountains to find them. There is an increasing exactness and care in finish, as his works progressed.

The decade from 1870 to 1880 was a busy one for this author, not only in his home study, in the Boston libraries, but also with the pen and with voice. The formation of the Grand Army of the Republic, and the establishments of Posts all over the country, and especially in the Northern States, created a demand for lectures on the war. The soldiers themselves wished to study the great subject as a whole, while their wives and children and friends were only too glad to support the movement for the gathering of Post libraries, or the collection in the town public libraries of books relating to the war. The younger generation needed instruction as to causes, as well as to results. Carleton was everywhere a favorite, because of his personality, as well as of his wide and profound acquaintance, from actual observation, of the great movements which consolidated nations.

Years before becoming a war correspondent, Carleton had longed to be an orator who could sway thousands by the magic of his eloquence. More than once, after hearing Edward Everett, Rufus Choate, Wendell Phillips, and such masters of audiences, he would be unable to sleep, so excited was he by what he had heard, and still more by the power evinced in a single mind moving the wills of thousands. In such hours he longed to be a great orator, and thought no sacrifice too great to make in order to achieve success. As his own opportunities for public speaking multiplied, he became a fluent and convincing speaker, with clear ideas, picturesque language, and the power of dramatic antithesis. He had that gift of making pictures to the mind by which a speaker can turn the ears of his auditors into eyes. His tall form, luminous face, impressive sincerity, and contagious earnestness made delighted hearers, especially among the soldiers, who everywhere hailed him as their defender, their faithful historian, and their steadfast friend. To take the hand of Carleton, after his address or lecture, was a privilege for which men and women strove as a high honor, and which children, now grown men and women, remember for a lifetime.

Nevertheless, in the sound judgment of the critic, Carleton would not be reckoned, as he himself knew well, in the front rank of orators. Neither in overmastering grace of person, in power of unction, in magnetic conquest of the mind and will, was he preëminent. When, leaving the flowery meadows of description or rising from the table-land of noble sentiment and inspiring precepts, he attempted to rise in soaring eloquence, his oratorical abilities did not match the grandeur of his thought or the splendor of his diction.

In the course of his career as a speaker, he delivered at least two thousand lectures and addresses on formal occasions, besides unnumbered offhand speeches. Being one of those full men, it was of him that it could be said, *Semper paratus.* On whatever subject he

spoke, he was sure to make it interesting.
Besides reports of his addresses and orations
in the newspapers, several of the most important have been published in pamphlet form.
At the centennial celebration at Boscawen,
N. H., on the 4th of July, and at the 45th
anniversary of the settlement of Rev. Edward
Buxton, at the 50th anniversary of the Histor-
ical-Genealogical Society of Boston, and at
Nantucket, before the Bostonian Society and
at the Congregational Clubs, before Press Associations, Legislative and Congressional Committees, on Social and Labor questions, and at
the Congress held in Chicago for the promotion of international commerce between the
countries of North and South America, Carleton reached first an audience, and then, through
the types, wider circles of readers.

CHAPTER XXII

BESIDES other means of recreation, Carleton was happy in having been from childhood a lover of music. In earlier life he sang in the church choir, under the training of masters of increasing grades of skill, in his native village, at Malden, and in Boston. He early learned to play upon keyed instruments, the melodion, the piano, and the organ, the latter being his favorite. From this great encyclopædia of tones, he loved to bring out grand harmonies. He used this instrument of many potencies, for enjoyment, as a means of culture, for the soothing of his spirits, and the resting of his brain. When wearied with the monotony of work with his pen, he would leave his study, as I remember, when living in Boston, and, having a private key to Shawmut Church, and dependent on no assistance except that of the water-motor, he would, for a half hour or more, and sometimes for hours, delight and refresh himself with this organ, — grandest of all but one, in Boston, the city of good organs and organ-makers. Many times throughout the war, in churches deserted or occupied, alone or in the public service, in the soldier's camp-church or meeting in the open air, wherever there was an instrument with keys, Carleton was a valued participant and aid in worship.

Religious music was his favorite, but he delighted in all sweet melodies. He loved the Boston Symphony concerts and the grand opera. Among his best pieces of writing were the accounts of Wagner's Parsifal at Bayreuth, and the great Peace Jubilee after our civil war. At most of the great musical events in Boston, he was present.

Shawmut Church had for many years one of the very best quartette choirs in the city, supported at the instrument by such organists as Dudley Buck, George Harris, Samuel Carr, H. E. Parkhurst, and Henry M. Dunham. In Carleton, both voice and instrument found so appreciative a hearer, and one who so often personally commended or appraised their renderings of a great composer's thought, or a heart-touching song, that " as well the singers as the players on instruments " were always glad to know how he received their art and work.   In Europe, this lover of sweet sound enjoyed hearing the greatest vocalists, and those mightiest of the masses of harmony known on earth, and possible only in European capitals.   Before going to some noble feast for ear and soul, as, for example, Wagner's rendition of his operas at Bayreuth, Carleton would study carefully the literary history, the ideas sought to be expressed in sound, and the score of the composer.   In his grand description and interpretation of Parsifal, he likened it among operas to the Jungfrau amid the Bernese Alps.   " In its sweep of vision, beauty, greatness, whiteness, glory, and grandeur, it stands alone . . . to show the greatness, the ideal of Wagner, including the conflict of all time, — the upbuilding of individual character, — and reaching on to eternity."

Carleton, being a real Christian, necessarily believed in, and heartily supported, foreign missionary work.   He saw in his Master, Christ, the greatest of all missionaries, and in the twelve missionaries, whom he chose to carry on his work, the true order and line of the kingdom. "Apostolical" succession is, literally, and in Christ's intent, missionary succession. He read in Paul's account of the organization of the Christian Church, that, among its orders and dignities, its officers and personnel, were "first missionaries." To him the only "orders" and "succession" were those which propagated the Gospel. He had seen the work of the modern apostles, sent forth by American Christians, west of the Alleghanies first, west of the Mississippi. He had later beheld the true apostles at work, in India, China, and Japan. It was on account of his seeing that he became a still more enthusiastic upholder of missionary, or apostolic, work. He gave many addresses and lectures in New England, in loyalty to the mind of the Master. As he had been a friend of the black man, slave or free, so also was he ever a faithful defender of the Asiatic stranger within our gates. Against the bill which practically excluded the Chinamen from the United States, in defiance of the spirit and letter of the Burlingame treaty, Carleton spoke vigorously, at the meeting held in Tremont Temple, in

Boston, to protest against the infamous Exclusion bill, which committed the nation to perjury. Carleton could never see the justice of stealing black men from Africa to enslave them, of murdering red men in order to steal their hunting-grounds, or of inviting yellow men across the sea to do our work, and then kicking them out when they were no longer needed.

Carleton was instrumental in giving impetus to the movement to found that mission in Japan which has since borne fruit in the creation of the largest and most influential body of Christian churches, and the great Doshisha University, in Kioto. These churches are called Kumi-ai, or associated independent churches, and out of them have come, in remarkable numbers, preachers, pastors, editors, authors, political leaders, and influential men in every department of the new modern life in Japan. It was at the meeting of the American Board, held in Pittsburg, in the Third Presbyterian Church edifice, October 7-8, 1869, that the mission to Japan was proposed. A paper by Secretary Treat was read, and reported on favorably, and Rev. David Greene, who had volunteered to be the apostle to the Sunrise Empire, made an address. The speech of Carleton, who had just returned from Dai Nippon, capped the climax of enthusiasm, and the meeting closed by singing the hymn, " Nearer, my God, to Thee."

At one of the later meetings of the Board, at Rutland, Vermont, the Japanese student Neesima pleaded effectually that a university be founded, the history of which, under the name of the One Endeavor, or Doshisha, is well known. In the same year that Neesima was graduated from Amherst College, Carleton received from this institution the honorary degree of Master of Arts.

Carleton could turn his nimble pen to rhyme, when his friends required verses, and best when his own emotions struggled for utterance in poetry. Several very creditable hymns were composed for anniversary occasions and for the Easter Festivals of Shawmut Church.

Indeed, the first money ever paid him by a publisher was for a poem,—" The Old Man's Meditations," which was copied into " Littell's Living Age." The pre-natal life, birth, and growth of this first-born child of Carleton's brain and heart, which inherited a "double portion," in both fame and pelf, is worth noting. In 1852, an aged uncle of Mrs. Coffin, who dwelt in thoughts that had not yet become the commonplace property of our day, being at home in the immensities of geology and the infinities of astronomy, made a visit to the home in Boscawen, spending some days. Carleton was richly fed in spirit, and, conceiving the idea of the poem, on going out to plough, put paper and pencil in his pocket. As he thought out line upon line, or stanza by stanza, he penned each in open air. At the end of the furrow, or even in the middle of it, he would stop his team, lay the paper on the back of the oxen, and write down the thought or line. Finished at home in the evenings, the poem was read to a friend, who persuaded the author to test its editorial and mercantile value.

"I shall never forget," wrote Mrs. Coffin, October 13, 1896, "with what joy he came to me and showed me the poetry in the magazine, and a check for $5.00."

The last three stanzas are :

" He sails once more the sea of years
    So wide and vast and deep !
He lives anew old hopes and fears —
Sweet tales of love again he hears,
While flow afresh the scalding tears,
    For one long since asleep.

" He sees the wrecks upon the shore,
    And everything is drear ;
The rolling waves around him roar,
The angry clouds their torrents pour,
His friends are gone forevermore,
    And he alone is here.

" Yet through the gloom of gathering night,
    A glory from afar
Streams ever on his fading sight,
With Orient beams that grow more bright,
The dawn of heaven's supernal light
    From Bethlehem's radiant star."

During the evenings of 1892, Carleton
guided a Reading Club of young ladies who
met at his house. I remember, one evening,
with what effect he read Lowell's " Biglow
Papers," his eyes twinkling with the fun which
none enjoyed more than he. On another
evening, after reading from Longfellow's "The
Poet's Tale," " Lady Wentworth," and other

poems, Carleton, before retiring, wrote a " Sequel to Lady Wentworth." It is full of drollery, suggesting also what might possibly have ensued if " the judge " had married " Maud Müller." Carleton's poem tells of the risks and dangers to marital happiness which the old magistrate runs who weds a gay young girl.

Carleton was ever a lover and student of poetry, and among poets, Whittier was from the first his favorite. As a boy he committed to memory many of the Quaker poet's trumpet-like calls to duty. As a man he always turned for inspiration to this sweet singer of freedom. What attracted Carleton was not only the intense moral earnestness of the Friend, his beautiful images and grand simplicity, but the seer's perfect familiarity with the New Hampshire landscape, its mountains, its watercourses, the ways and customs of the people, the local legends and poetical associations, the sympathy with the Indian, and the seraphic delight which he took in the play of light upon the New Hampshire hills. Not more did Daniel Webster study with eager eyes the glowing and the paling of the light on the hilltops, no more rapturously did Rembrandt unweave the mazes of darkness, conjure the shadows, and win by study the mysteries of light and shade, than did Whittier. To Carleton, a true son of New Hámpshire, who had himself so often in boyhood watched and discriminated the mystery-play of light in its variant forms at dawn, midday, and sunset, by moon and star and zodiac, at the equinoxes and solstices, the imagery of his favorite poet was a perennial delight.

As he ripened in years, Carleton loved poetry more and more. He delighted in Lowell, and enjoyed the mysticism of Emerson. He had read Tennyson earlier in life without much pleasure, but in ripened years, and with refined tastes, his soul of music responded to the English bard's marvellous numbers. He became unspeakably happy over the tender melody of Tennyson's smaller pieces, and the grand harmony of "In Memoriam," which he thought the greatest poem ever written, and the high-water mark of intellect in the nineteenth century. Carleton was not only a lover of music, but a composer. When some especially tender sentiment in a hymn impressed him, or the re-reading of an old sacred song kindled his imagination by its thought, or moved his sensibilities by its smooth rhythm, then Carleton was not likely to rest until he had made a tune of his own with which to express his feelings. Of the scores which he composed and sang at home, or had sung in the churches, a number were printed, and have had happy use.

To the end of his life, he seemed to present, in his carriage and person, some of that New Hampshire ruggedness, and even rustic simplicity, that attracted and lured, while it foiled and disgusted those hunters of human prey who, in every large city, wait to take in the wayfaring man, whether he be fool or wise. Because he wore comfortable shoes, and cared next to nothing about conformity to the last new freak of fashion, the bunco man was very apt to make a fool of himself, and find that he, and not the stranger, was the victim. In Boston, which of late years has been so far captured by the Irishman that even St. Patrick's is celebrated under the guise of " Evacuation Day," matters were not very different from those in New York. Carleton, while often conducting parties of young friends around Copp's Hill, and the more interesting historical, but now uncanny houses of the North End, was often remarked. Occasionally he was recognized by the policeman, who would inform suspicious or inquiring fellow foreigners or adopted sons of the Commonwealth, that "the old fellow was only a countryman in town, and wouldn't do any harm."

Lest some might get a false idea, I need only state that Mr. Coffin was a man of dignified dress, and scrupulously neat. He was a gentleman whose engaging presence might suggest the older and more altruistic, rather than the newer and perhaps brusquer style of manners. His was a " mild and magnificent " blue eye in which so many, who loved him so, liked to dwell, and he had no need to wear glasses. The only sign of ornament about him was his gold watch-chain and cross-bar in his black vest button-hole.

CHAPTER XXIII

SHAWMUT CHURCH

SHAWMUT Church, in Boston, stands at the corner of Tremont and Brookline Streets. Its history is one of unique interest. Its very name connects the old and new world together. A Saxon monk, named Botolph, after completing his Christian studies in Germany, founded, A. D. 654, a monastery in Lincolnshire, on the Witham, near the sea, and made it a centre of holy light and knowledge. He was the friend of sailors and boat-folk. The houses which grew up around the monastery became Botolph's Town, or Boston. " Botolph " is itself but another form of boat-help, and the famous tower of this English parish church, finer than many cathedrals, is crowned by an octagon lantern, nearly three hundred feet above the ground. It serves as a beacon-light, being visible forty miles distant, and, as of old, is the boat-help of Saint Botolph's

Town. This ecclesiastical lighthouse is familiarly called " Boston Stump," and overlooks Lincolnshire, the cradle of Massachusetts history. At Scrooby, a few miles to the west, lived and worshipped the Pilgrim Fathers and Mothers. From this shire, also, came the English people who settled at Shawmut on the 17th of September, 1630.

The Indian name, Shawmut, was that of the " place near the neck," [1] probably the present Haymarket Square. The three-hilled peninsula called Tremont, or Boston, by the white settlers, was connected with the main land at Roxbury by a long, narrow neck or causeway. The future " South End " was then under the waves. After about two centuries of use as a wagon road, this narrow strip between Boston and Roxbury — so narrow that, at high tide, boys were able to leap from the foam of the South Bay to the spray of the waters of the Charles River — was widened. Suffolk Street, which was one of the first highways west of Washington Street to be made into hard ground, was named Shawmut Avenue. About the

---

[1] Other good authorities interpret Shawmut as meaning "living waters."

middle of the nineteenth century, much land was reclaimed from the salt mud and marshes and made ready for the pile-driver, mason, and builder. Two splendid districts, the first called the " South End," and the second the " Back Bay," were created. Where, in the Revolutionary War, British frigates lay at anchor, are now Beacon Street and Commonwealth and Massachusetts Avenues. Where the redcoats stepped into their boats for disembarkation at the foot of Bunker Hill, stretch the lovely Public Gardens. The streets running east and west in the new districts, beginning with Dover and ending with Lenox, are named after towns in the Bay State. About midway among these, as to order and distance, are Brookline and Canton Streets.

On a chance space of hard soil around Canton and Dedham Streets, in this marshy region, a suburban village of frame houses had gathered, and here a Sunday school was started as early as 1836. In January, 1842, a weekly prayer-meeting began at the house of Mr. Samuel C. Wilkins. On November 20, 1845, a church was formed, with fifty members. In the newly filled up land, the pile-driver was already busy in planting forests of full-grown trees head downward. All around were rising blocks of elegant houses, with promise of imposing civic and ecclesiastical edifices of various kinds. In the wider streets were gardens, parks, or ample strips of flower-beds. This was the land of promise, and into it pressed married couples by the hundreds, creating lovely homes, rearing families, and making this the choicest part of the young city. For, though " Boston town " is as old as Mother Goose's rhymes, the municipality of Boston was, in 1852, but thirty years old. The congregation of Christian people which, on April 14, 1849, took the name, as parish, of The Shawmut Congregational Society, and, as a church, one month later, the name of the Shawmut Congregational Church, occupied as a meeting-house first a hall, then a frame building, and finally a handsome edifice of brick, which was dedicated on the 18th of November, 1852. This building is now occupied by the Every Day Church, of the Universalist denomination. The tide of prosperity kept steadily rising. The throng of worshippers increased, until, in the very midst of the great Civil War,

it was necessary to have more room. The
present grand edifice on Tremont Street was
erected and dedicated February 11, 1864;
the Rev. Edwin Bonaparte Webb, who had
been called from Augusta, Maine, being the
popular and successful pastor.

Boston was not then noted, as she certainly
is now, for grandeur or loveliness in church
edifices.   Neither excellence nor taste in ecclesiastical architecture was, before the war, a striking trait of the city or the people.   To-day her
church spires and towers are not only numerous,
but are famed for their variety and beauty.

Fortunately for the future of Boston, the
people of Shawmut Church found a good archi-
tect, who led the van of improvement in church
architecture.   The new edifice was the first one
in the city on the early Lombardy style of
architecture, and did much to educate the taste
of the people of the newer and the older town,
and especially those in the fraternity of churches
called Congregational.

Both its architecture and decoration have
been imitated and improved upon in the city
wherein it was a pioneer of beauty and the
herald of a new order of church architecture.

It is a noble vehicle of the faith and feelings of devout worshippers.

The equipment of Shawmut Church edifice made it a very homelike place of worship, and here, for a generation or more of Carleton's life, a noble company of Christians worshipped. The Shawmut people were noted for their enterprise, sociability, generosity, and unity of purpose. In this "South End" of Boston was reared a large proportion of the generation which to-day furnishes the brain and social and religious force of the city and suburbs. In Shawmut Church, gathered, week by week, hundreds of those who, in the glow of prosperity, held common ambitions, interests, and hopes. They were proud of their city, their neighborhood, and their church, yet were ever ready to extend their well-laden hands in gifts to the needy at home, and to send to those far off, within our own borders, and in lands beyond sea.

The great fire in Boston, of which Carleton wrote so brilliant a description, which, beginning November 9, 1872, within a few hours burned over sixty-five acres and reduced seventy-five millions of property to smoke and ashes, gave the first great blow to the material prosperity of Shawmut Church. Later came the filling up, the reclamation, and building of the Back Bay district. About 1878, the tide of movement set to the westward, progressing so rapidly and steadily as to almost entirely change, within a decade, the character of the South End, from a region of homes to one largely of business and boarding houses. Still later, about 1890, with the marvellous development of the electric motor and trolley cars, making horse traction by rail obsolete, the suburbs of Boston became one great garden and a semicircle of homes. Then Brookline, Newton, and Dorchester churches flourished at the expense of the city congregations. Shawmut Church, having graduated hundreds of families, had, in 1893, to be reorganized.

Of this church Charles Carleton Coffin, though not one of the founders, was certainly one of the makers. As a member, a hearer, a worshipper, a teacher, an officer, a counsellor, a giver of money, power, and influence, his name is inseparably associated with the life of Shawmut Church.

When Carleton's seat was vacant, the chief

servant of the church knew that his faithful ally was serving his Master elsewhere. After one of his trips to Europe, out West, or down South over the old battle-fields, to refresh his memory, or to make notes and photographs for his books, the welcome given to him, on his return, was always warm and lively.

First of all, Mr. Coffin was a good listener. This man, so fluent in speech, so ready with his pen, so richly furnished by long and wide reading, and by habitual meditation and deep thinking, by unique experience of times that tried men's souls, knew also the moments when silence, that is golden, was better than speech, even though silvern. These were not as the " brilliant flashes of silence," such as Sidney Smith noted as delightful improvements in his friend " Tom " Macaulay ; for Carleton was never a monopolist in conversation. Rather, with the prompting of a generous nature, and as studied courtesy made into fine art, he could listen even to a child. If Carleton was present, the preacher had an audience. His face, while beaming with encouragement, was one of singular responsiveness. His patience, the patience of one to whom concealment of feeling was as difficult as for a crystal to shut out light, rarely failed.

In Japan there are temples, built *in memoriam* to heroes fallen in war. These are named Shrines for the Welcome of Spirits. They are lighted at sunset. Like one of these that I remember, called the Soul-beckoning Rest, was this listener, Carleton, who begat eloquence by his kindly gaze. Nor was this power to lift up and cheer — this winged help of a great soul, like that of a mother bird under her fledgling making first trial of the air — given only to the professional speaker in the pulpit. This ten-talent layman was ever kindly helpful, with ear and tongue, to his fellow holder-in-trust of the one, or of the five, talents; yes, even to the little children in Christ's kingdom.

The young people loved Carleton because he heard and loved them. To have his great, kindly eyes fixed on some poor soldier, or neighbor in distress, was in itself a lightening of the load of trouble. Unlike those professional or volunteer comforters, who overwhelm by dumping a whole cart-load of condolence upon the sufferer, who is unable to resist or reply, Carleton was often great in his power of encouraging silence, and of gentle sympathy.

Bacon, as no other Englishman, has compressed in very few words a recipe for making a "full," a "ready," and an "exact" man. Carleton was all these in one. He was ever full. In the Shawmut prayer-meeting, his deep, rich voice was the admirable vehicle of his strong and helpful thoughts. Being a man of intense conviction, there was earnestness in every tone. A stalwart in faith, he was necessarily optimistic. A prophet, he was always sure that out of present darkness was to break forth grander light than former days knew. This world is governed by our Father, and God makes no mistakes.

That rhetorical instrument, the historical present, which makes the pages of his books tell such vivid stories, he often used with admirable effect in the prayer-room, impressing and thrilling all hearts. No little one ever believed more confidently the promises of its parent than did this little child in humility who was yet a man in understanding. Yet his was not blind credulity. He always faced the facts. He was willing to get to the bottom of reality,

even though it might cause much drilling of
the strata, with revelation of things at first un-
pleasant to know.   I never knew a man whose
piety rested less on traditions, institutions, persons, things, or reputations taken for granted.
To keen intuitions, he was able to add the riches
of experience, and his experience ever wrought
hope.   Hence the tonic of his thought and
words.   He dwelt on the mountain-top of
vision, and yet he had that combination, so rare,
yet so indispensable in the prophet, — vision
and patience, even the patience of service.

Naturally his themes and his illustrations, so
pertinent and illuminating, were taken largely
from history.   It is because he saw so far and
so clearly down the perspective of the past, that
he read the future so surely.   "That which
hath been, is that which shall be," — but more.
"God fulfils himself in many ways."   To our
friend, history, of which the cross of Christ was
the centre, was the Heavenly Father's fullest
revelation.   Many are the ways of theophany,
— "at sundry times, and in divers manners,"
— to one the burning bush, to another the
Urim and Thummin, to another the dew on
the fleece, to one this, to another that.   To

our man of the Spirit, as to the sage of Patmos, human history, because moved from above, was the visible presence of God.

The war, which dissolved the old world of slavery, sectional bigotry, and narrow ideals, and out of the mother liquid of a new chaos shot forth fresh axes of moral reconstruction, furnished this soldier of righteousness with endless themes, incidents, illustrations, and suggestions. Yet the emphasis, both as to light and shading, was put upon things Christian and Godlike, the phenomena of spiritual courage and enterprise, rather than upon details of blood or slaughter. Neither years nor distance seemed to dim our fellow patriot's gratitude to the brave men who sacrificed limb and life for their country. The soldierly virtues, so vital to the Christian, were brought home to heart and conscience. He showed the incarnation of truth and life to be possible even in the camp and field.

Having been a skilled traveller in the Holy Land, Carleton frequently opened this " Fifth Gospel " to delighted listeners. There hung on the wall of the " vestry," or social prayer-room, above the leader's chair, a steel-plate picture of modern Jerusalem, showing especially the walls, gates, and roadways leading out from the city. Carleton often declared that this print was " an inspiration " to him. It recalled not only personal experiences of his own journeys, but also the stirring incidents in Scripture, especially of the life of Christ. Having studied on the soil of Syria, the background of the parables, and possessing a genius for topography, he was able to unshackle our minds from too close bondage to the English phrase or letter, from childhood's imperfect imaginations, and from our crude Occidental fancies. Many a passage of Scripture, long held in our minds as the hand holds an un-lighted lantern, was often turned into an immediately helpful lamp to our path by one touch of his light-giving torch.

For many years, Carleton was a Bible-class teacher, excelling in understanding, insight, explanation, and application of the divine Word. Many to-day remember his teaching powers and their enjoyment at Malden ; but it was in Boston, at Shawmut Church, that Mr. Coffin gave to this work the fullness of his strength and the ripeness of his powers.

Counting it one of the noblest ambitions of

a man's life to be a good teacher, I used to admire Carleton's way of getting at the heart of the lesson. His talent lay in first drawing out the various views of the readers, and then of harmonizing them, — even as the lens draws all rays to a burning-point, making fire where before was only scattered heat. Carleton was one of those superb teachers who believe that education is not only putting in, but also drawing out. In his class were lawyers, physicians, doctors of divinity, principals of schools, heads of families, besides various specimens of average humanity. Somehow, he contrived, within the scant hour afforded him, often within a half hour, to bestow not only his own thought, but, by powerful spiritual induction, to kindle in others a transforming force. After the teaching had well begun, there set in an alternating current of intensity that wrought mightily for the destruction of dead prejudices, and the building up of character.

In his use of helps and commentaries he had a profound contempt of those peddlers of pedantry who try to make the words of eternal truth become merely the lingo of things local and temporary. He was fond of utilizing all that

the spade has cast up and out from the earth,
as well as of consulting what the pen of genius
has made so plain.   He believed heartily in
that interpretive, or higher criticism, which has
done so much in our days to open the riches
of holy Scripture.   From the very first, instead
of fearing that truth might be injured by an
examination of the dress in which it was clothed,
or the packages in which it was wrapped, Carleton was in hearty sympathy with those scholars
and investigators who, by the application of
literary canons to the Hebrew and Greek writ-
ings, have put illuminating difference between
traditions and the original message.   He believed that, in the popular understanding of
many portions of the Bible, there was much
confusion, owing to the webs which have been
spun over the text by men who lived centuries
and ages after the original writers of the inspired word.   Though he never called himself
a scholar, he knew only too well that Flavius
Josephus and John Milton were the makers of
much popular tradition which ascribed to the
Bible a good deal which it does not contain,
and that there was often difficulty among the
plain people in distinguishing between the an-

cient treasure and the wrapping and strings within which it is now enclosed. Hence his diligent use of some of the strong books in his pastor's and other libraries.

Above all, however, was his own clear, penetrating, spiritual insight, which, joined with his rich experience, his literary instincts, and his own gift of expression, made him such a master in the art of communication. While his first use of the Bible was for spiritual benefit to himself and others, he held that its study as literature would scatter to the wind the serious objections of sceptics and unbelievers.

CHAPTER XXIV

THE FREE CHURCHMAN

CARLETON was a typical free churchman. He was not only so by inheritance and environment, but because he was master of the New Testament. His penetrating acumen and power to read rightly historical documents enabled him to see what kind of churches they were which the apostles founded. With the open New Testament before him, he did not worry himself about the validity of the ordination of those who should preach to him or administer the sacraments, though there was no more loyal churchman and Christian. He believed in the kind of churches which were first formed at Jerusalem and in the Roman cities by the twelve whom Jesus chose, over which not even the apostles themselves ventured to exercise authority; but rather, on the other hand, submitted to the congregation, that is, the assembled believers. In the New Testament, Carleton read that the members of the churches were on the same level, all being equal before their great Head and risen Lord, no member having the smallest claim to any kind of authority over or among his fellow members. In such churches, organized to-day as closely as possible after the New Testament model, he believed, and to such churches he gave his heartiest support, while ever deeply sympathetic with his fellow Christians who associated themselves under other methods of government.

His strong faith in the essential right and truth held by independent churches in fraternity, never wavered; and this faith received even increasing strength because of his trust in human nature when moved from above. He believed in the constant presence of the Holy Spirit, as leading Christians unto the way of all truth. He thought the centuries to come would see a shedding off of many things dogmatic theologians consider to be vital to Christianity, and the closer apprehension by society of the meaning of Christ's life and words. He believed not only that God was, but that he is. Though reared in New England, he had

little of that provincial narrowness which so
often mars and cramps the minds of those who
otherwise are the most agreeable of all Americans, — the cultivated New Englanders. No
sermon so moved Carleton, and so kindled
responsive radiance in his face, as those which
showed that God is to-day leading and guiding
humanity and individuals as surely as in the
age of the burning bush or the smoking altar.
He believed that neither the ancient Jews nor
the early Christians had any advantages over
us for spiritual culture, or for the foundation
and increase of their faith in God, but rather
less. He heartily approved of whatever pierced
sectarian shams and traditional hypocrisies and
revealed reality.

Hence his coolness and impartiality in controversy, whatever might be his own strong
personal liking. His profound knowledge of
human nature in all its forms, not excepting
the clerical, professional, and theological sort,
— especially when in the fighting mood, — enabled him to measure accurately the personal
equation in every problem, even when masked
to the point of self-deception. His judicial
balance and his power to see the real point in

a controversy made him an admirable guide, philosopher, and friend. His vital rather than traditional view and use of the truth, and his sunny calm and poise, were especially manifested during that famous period of trouble which broke out in that noble but close corporation, the American Board of Commissioners for Foreign Missions.

Through all the subsidiary skirmishes connected with the prosecution of the Andover professors, and the great debates in the public meetings of the American Board, Carleton was in hearty sympathy with those opinions and convictions which have since prevailed. He was in favor of sending men and women into missionary fields who showed, by their physical, intellectual, and spiritual make-up, that they were fitted for their noble work, whether or not their theology stood the test of certain arbitrary standards in vogue with a faction in a close corporation.

Carleton was never averse to truth being tried on a fair field, whether of discussion, of controversy before courts, or, if necessary, at the rifle's muzzle. He was not one of those feeble souls who retreat from all agitation.

He had once fronted " a lie in arms " and was accustomed to probe even an angel's professions. He knew that in the history of man there must often be a storm before truth is revealed in clearness. No one realized more fully than he that, among the evangelical churches holding the historic form of Christianity, the part ever played and perhaps yet to be played by Congregationalists, is that of pioneers. He knew that out of the bosom of this body of Christians had come very many of the great leaders of thought who have so profoundly modified Christian theology in America and Europe, and that by Congregationalists are written most of the books shaping the vanguard of thought in America, and he rejoiced in the fact.

In brief, Charles Carleton Coffin was neither a " mean Yankee," nor, in his general spirit, a narrow New Englander. He was not a local, but a genuinely national American and free churchman. He believed that the idea of the people ruling in the Church as well as in the State had a historical, but not absolutely necessary, connection with New England. In his view, the Congregational form of a church government was as appropriate to the Middle and Western States of our country, as to the six Eastern States. Ever ready to receive new light and to ponder a new proposition, he grew and developed, as the years went on, in his conception of the origin of Congregational Christianity in apostolic times, and of its re-birth after the release of the Bible from its coffin of dead Latin and Greek into the living tongues of Europe, among the so-called Ana-baptists. Through his researches he had long suspected that those Christians, whom prelates and political churchmen had, besides murdering and attempting to exterminate, so vilified and misrepresented, were our spiritual ancestors and the true authors in modern time of church government through the congregation, and of freedom of the conscience in religion. He often spoke of that line of succession of thought and faith which he saw so clearly traced through the Lollards and the weavers of eastern England, the Dutch Anabaptists, the Brownists, and the Pilgrims. He gave his hearty adherence to what he believed to be the demonstration of the truth as set forth in an article in *The New World*, by the writer, in the

following letter, written February 27, 1896,
only four days before his sudden death and
among the very last fruits of his pen. Like
the editor who prints "letters from correspondents," the biographer is "not responsible
for the opinions expressed."

ALWINGTON, 9 SHAILER STREET,
BROOKLINE, MASS.

DEAR DR. GRIFFIS : — I have read your Anabaptist article,
— once for my own meditation, and once for Mrs. Coffin's
benefit. I am glad you have shown up Motley, and that
toleration did not begin with Roger Williams. Your article
historically will dethrone two saints, — Williams and Lord
Baltimore. You have rendered an invaluable service to history. Our Baptist and Catholic brethren will not thank
you, but the rest of the world will. It is becoming clearer
every day that the motive force which was behind the foun-
dations of this Republic came from the " Lollards " and the
" Beggars." I hope you will give us more such articles.

Having been for many years an active member of the Congregational Club, of Boston,
Carleton was in 1890 elected president, and
served during one year. This parent of the
fifty or more Congregational Clubs scattered
throughout the country was organized in 1869,
and has had an eventful history of power and in-

fluence. Some of the topics discussed during his administration were " Relations of the Church to Politics," " Congregationalism in Boston," " Bible Class Study," and " How shall the Church adapt itself to modern needs?" It was under his presidency, also, that the Boston Congregational Club voted unanimously, February 24, 1890, to appoint a committee to obtain the necessary funds and erect a memorial at Delfshaven in honor of the Dutch Republicans and the Pilgrim Fathers, — both hosts and guests. When the suggestion to raise some such memorial, made by the Hon. S. R. Thayer, American Minister at the Hague, was first read in the meeting of the Club in October, 1889, and a motion made to refer it to the Executive Committee, Carleton seconded and supported the motion with a speech in warm commendation. He was among the very first to make and pay a subscription in money. The enterprise still awaits the happy day of completion, and the responsibility of the enterprise lies, by its own vote, upon the Boston Congregational Club. The Forefathers' Day celebration of the Club was of uncommon interest during the year of Mr. Coffin's presidency.

A leading feature was the display on a screen of views of Pilgrim shrines in England which Mr. Coffin had obtained on a visit two years before.

Except his membership in the various historical and learned societies and in religious organizations, Mr. Coffin was not connected with secret, benevolent, social, or mysterious brotherhoods. He did not believe in secret fraternities, but rather considered that these had much to do with weakening the Church of Christ, and with making men satisfied with a lower standard of ethics and human sociability than that taught by Jesus. He held that the brotherhood instituted of Christ, in an open chapter of twelve, and without secrets of any kind, was sufficient for him and for all men. More than once, when going abroad, or travelling in the various parts of his own country, which is nearly as large as all Europe, he was advised to join a lodge and unite himself with one or more of the best secret fraternities, for assistance and recognition while travelling. All these kind invitations he steadily declined. He was not even a member of the Grand Army of the Republic, though often invited to join a Post. He never became a member, for he did not see the necessity of secrecy, even for this organization, though he was very often an honored guest at their public meetings. The Church of Christ was to Carleton an all-sufficient society and power.

CHAPTER XXV

ONE can hardly imagine a better school for the training of a good American citizen than that which Carleton enjoyed. By inheritance and birth in a New Hampshire village, he knew " the springs of empire." By actual experience of farming and surveying in a transition era between the old ages of manual labor and the new æon of inventions, he learned toil, its necessity, and how to abridge and guide it by mind. In the acquaintance, while upon a Boston newspaper, with public men, and all kinds of people, in the unique experiences as war correspondent, in wide travel and observation around the whole world, in detailed studies of new lands and life in the Northwest, in reading and research in great libraries, and in the constant discipline of his mind through reflection, his knowledge of man and nature, of society and history, was at first hand.

Intensely interested in politics from boyhood, Carleton sought no public office.

When, in his early manhood, he revolved in his mind the question of attempting this or that career, he may have thought of entering the alluring but thorny path of office-seeking and "practical" politics. It cannot be said that his desire for public emolument lasted very long. He deliberately decided against a political career. Even if the exigencies of the moment had not tended to forbid the flight of his ambition in this direction, there were other reasons against it.

He was a school commissioner in Malden, faithfully attending to the details of his duty during two years. The report of his work was given in a pamphlet. As we have seen, before the breaking out of the war, when in Washington, he sought for a little while government employment in one of the departments, but gave up the quest when the larger field of war correspondent invited him. He never sought an elective office, but when his fellow citizens in Boston found out how valuable a member of the Commonwealth he was, so rich in public spirit and so well equipped to be a legislator,

he was made first, for several terms, a Representative, and afterwards, for one term, a Senator,
in the Legislature of Massachusetts. Carleton
sat under the golden codfish as Representative
during the years 1884 and 1885, and under the
gilded dome as Senator, in 1890.

Faithful to his calling as a maker of law,
Carleton was abundant in labors during his
three terms, interested in all that meant weal
or woe to the Commonwealth; yet we have
only room to speak of the two or three particular reforms which he inaugurated.

Until the year 1884, Boston was behind
some of the other cities of the Union, notably
Philadelphia, in requiring the children in the
public schools to provide their own text-books.
This caused the burden of taxation for education, which is "the chief defence of nations,"
to fall upon the men and women who reared
families, instead of being levied with equal
justice upon all citizens. Carleton prepared a
bill for furnishing free text-books to the public
schools of Boston, such as had been done in
Philadelphia since 1819. Despite considerable
opposition, some of it on the part of teachers
who had severe notions,— bred chiefly by local

Boston precedent, which had almost the force of religion, — Carleton had the happiness of seeing the bill passed.

The administration of municipal affairs in the " Hub of the Universe," during the seventies and early eighties of this proud century, was one not at all creditable to any party nor to the city that prides itself on being distinctive and foremost in fame. The development of political life in New England had been after the model of the town. Municipal organization was not looked upon with much favor until well into this century. While the population of the Middle States was advancing in the line of progress in government of cities, the people in the Eastern States still clung to the model of the town meeting as the perfection of political wisdom and practice. This was done in the case of Boston, even when several tens of thousands of citizens, dwelling as one political union, made the old system antiquated.

Before the opening of the 19th century, all the municipally incorporated cities of the Northern United States, excepting Albany, lay along a line between the boundaries of Manhattan Island and Philadelphia. It was not until

1830 that " Boston town " became a city.
For fifty years afterwards, the development of
municipal enterprise was in the direction of
superficial area, rather than according to foresight or genius.   It is very certain that the
fathers of that epoch did not have a very clear
idea of, certainly did not plan very intelligently
for, the vast growth of our half of the century.
Added to this ultra conservatism, came the
infusion, with attendant confusion, of Ireland's
sons and daughters by myriads, a flood of
Scotch-Irish and other nationalities from Canada, and the flocking of large numbers of native
Americans from the rural districts of New
England.   Nearly all of the newcomers usually arrived poor and with intent to become
rich as quickly as honesty would allow, while
not a few were without limit of time or scruple
of conscience to hinder their plans.   The
Americans of "culture and character" were
usually too busy in making money and getting
clothes, houses, and horses, to attend to "politics," while Patrick was only too glad and
ready to develop his political abilities.   So it
came to pass that a ring of powerful political
" bosses " — if we may degrade so good and

honest a Dutch word — was formed. Saloons, gambling-houses and dance-halls multiplied, while an oligarchy, ever grasping for more power, nullified the laws and trampled the statutes under its feet. The sins of drunkenness and bribery among policemen, who were simply the creatures for the most part of corrupt politicians, were too frequent to attract much notice. That conscientious wearer of the blue and the star who enforced the laws was either discharged or sent on some unimportant suburban beat. The relations between city saloons and politics were as close as hand and glove, palm and coin. The gambler, the saloon-keeper, the masters of houses of ill-fame, were all in favor of the kind of municipal government which Boston had had for a generation or more.

An American back is like the camel's, — able to bear mighty loads, but insurgent at the last feather. So, in Boston, the long-outraged moral sense of the people suddenly revolted. A Citizens' Law and Order League was formed, and Charles Carleton Coffin, elected to the House of Representatives for the session of 1885, was asked to be their banner bearer in reform. With the idea of destroying partisanship and making the execution of the laws non-partisan, Carleton prepared a bill, which was intended to take the control of the police out of the hands of the Mayor and Common Council of the city, and to put it into the hands of the Governor of the Commonwealth.

When Mr. Coffin began this work, Boston had a population of 412,000 souls. From the "Boston bedrooms," that is, the suburban towns in five counties, one hundred thousand or more were emptied every day, making over half a million people. In this city there was an array of forces all massed against any legislation restricting their power, while eager and organized to extend it. These included 2,850 licensed liquor sellers, and 1,300 unlicensed places, besides 222 druggists; all of which, and whom, helped to make men drunk. To supply the thirsty there were within the city limits three distilleries and seventeen breweries. To show the nature of the oligarchy, we have only to state that there were twenty-five men who had their names as bondsmen on no fewer than 1,030 licenses, and that eight men signed the bonds of 610 licenses. These "bondsmen" of one sort controlled the votes of from

15,000 to 20,000 bondsmen of a lower sort.
The liquor business was then, as it is now, the
great incentive to lawlessness, helping to make
Boston a place of shame.   Ten thousand persons and $75,000,000 capital were employed
in work mostly useless and wicked.

"Boston's devil-fish was dragging her down."
The Sunday laws were set at defiance.   The
clinking of glasses could not only be distinctly
heard as one went by, but the streams of
young men openly filed in.   The laws, requiring a certain distance between the schoolhouse
and the saloon, were persistently violated.   Of
two hundred saloons visited by Carleton, one
hundred and twenty-eight had set the law at
defiance.   While six policemen were needed
in one Salvation Army room, to keep the
saints and sinners quiet, often there would be
not one star or club in the saloons.

Carleton began by arming himself with the
facts.   He visited hundreds of the tapster's
quarters in various parts of the city.   In some
cases he actually measured, with his own hands
and a surveyor's chain, the distance between
the schoolhouse and the home-destroyer.   He
talked with scores of policemen.   He then

prepared his bill and reported it in the Judiciary Committee, the members of which, about that time, received a petition in favor of a nonpartisan metropolitan board of police commissioners, in order to secure a much better enforcement of law. On this petition were scores of names, which the world will not willingly let die. Yet, after reading the petition, seven of the eleven members of the Committee were opposed to the bill, and so declared themselves. Carleton was therefore obliged to transfer the field of battle to the open House. When he counted noses in the Legislature, he found that in the double body there were but four men who were heartily in favor of the apparently unpopular reform. The bill lay dormant for many weeks. Almost as a matter of course, the Sunday newspapers were bitterly hostile to it. They informed their readers, more than once, that the reform was dead. By hostile politicians the bill was denounced as " infamous."

Nevertheless, the minority of four nailed their colors to the mast, " determined, if need be, to sink, but not to surrender." Behind them were the State constitution, the statutes of the General Court, and the whole history of Massachusetts, whose moral tonic has so often inspired the beginners of better times in American history. When the day came for discussion of the bill, in public, Mr. Coffin made a magnificent speech in its favor, March 17, 1885. Despite fierce opposition, the bill finally became law, creating a new era of hope and reform in the City on the Bay.

In a banquet given by the Citizens' Law and Order League, at the Hotel Vendome, to talk over the victory of law, about two hundred ladies and gentlemen were present. Among them were President Capen, of Tufts College, president of the League, and such grand citizens as Rufus Frost, Jonathan A. Lane, and Dr. Henry Martin Dexter; the Honorable Frank M. Ames, Senator, and Charles Carleton Coffin, Representative, being guests of honor. Carleton, being called upon for an address, said, among other things:

"There are no compensations in life more delightful and soul-satisfying than those which come from service and sacrifice for the welfare of our fellow men. . . . It has never troubled me to be in the minority. If you want real genuine pleasure in a battle, go in with the minority on some great principle affecting the we'fare of society."

In his speech he had said : " The moral sense of this community is a growing quantity, and no political party that ignores or runs counter to the lofty ideal can long stand before us."

The Honorable Alanson M. Beard had already paid a merited tribute when he said that Carleton had " lifted up this question above the domain of party politics into the higher realm of morals, where it belonged."

No one who knew Carleton need be told that, during all these weeks of uncertainty of issue, he was in constant prayer to God for light, guidance, and success. From all over the Commonwealth came letters of cheer and sympathy, especially from the mothers whose sons in Boston were tempted beyond measure because of the non-enforcement of law. To these, and to the law-loving editors of the newspaper press, the statesman afterwards returned his hearty thanks.

Carleton was a man ever open to conviction. To him, truth had no stereotyped forms. His mind never became a petrifaction, but was ever growing and vital.   At first he was opposed to civil service reform ; but after a study of the subject, he was convinced of its reasonableness and practicality, and became ever afterwards a hearty upholder of this method of selecting the servants of government, in the nation, the State, and the city.

He was a friend of woman suffrage.   On the occasion of a presentation of a petition from twenty thousand Massachusetts women, though four thousand of them had petitioned against the proposed measure, he made a strong and earnest plea for granting the ballot to women. Among other things he said : " No fire ever yet was lighted that could reduce to ashes an eternal truth."   He believed that women, as well as men, form society, and " the people, who were the true source, under God, of all authority on earth," were not made up wholly of one sex.   He quoted from that pamphlet, " De Jure Regni," published by George Buchanan in 1556, which was burned by the hangman in St. Paul's churchyard, — where so many Bibles and other good books have been burned, — which declared that " the will of the people is the only legitimate source of power."

He declared that the "lofty ideal of republicanism is the Sermon on the Mount." Of women,
he said, "Wherever they have walked, there
has been less of hell and more of heaven."

After an ex-mayor, in his speech, had referred
to Carleton's bill, which changed the appointing
power of the police from the Mayor and Common Council, and, by putting it in the hands of
the Governor and Executive Council, placed it
on the same foundation as the judiciary, as
"that infamous police law," Carleton said:
"Make a note of it, statesmen of the future.
Write it down in your memoranda, politicians
who indulge the expectation that you can ride
into power on the vices of society, — that moral
forces are marshalling as never before in the history of the human race, and that the women of
this country are beginning to wield them to
shape legislation on all great moral questions.
Refreshing as perfume-laden breezes from the
celestial plains were the words of encouragement
and sympathy that came to me from mothers
in Berkshire, from the Cape, from all over the
Commonwealth."

In 1890, in the Massachusetts Senate, there
was an attempt made to divide the town of

Beverly. Into this, as into so many of the pleasant towns, villages, and rural districts around Boston, wealthy Bostonians had come and built luxurious houses upon the land which they had bought. Not content with being citizens in the place where they were newcomers, — thus securing release from heavier taxes in Boston, where they lived in winter, — they wished to separate themselves, in a most un-American and un-democratic manner, from the older inhabitants and " common " people, and to make a new settlement with a separate local government for those who formed a particular class living in luxury. Carleton, hostile to the sordid and unsocial spirit lurking in the bill, vigorously opposed the attempted mutilation of an old historic town, and the isolation of " Beverly Farms." He opposed it, because it would be a bad precedent, and one in favor of class separation and class distinction. His speech embodies a masterly historical sketch of the town form of government.

CHAPTER XXVI

WHILE Carleton enjoyed that kind of work, ethical, literary, benevolent, and political, which appealed to sentiment and aroused sympathy to the burning point, he was an equally faithful coworker with God and man in enterprises wholly unsentimental. He who waits through eternity for his creatures to understand his own creation, knows how faithfully good men can coöperate with him in plans which only unborn and succeeding generations can appreciate.

Out of a thousand illustrations we may note, along the lines of electric science, the names of Professor Kinnersly, who probably first led Franklin into that line of research which enabled him to "snatch the sceptre from tyrants and the lightning from heaven," and Professor Moses Gerrish Farmer, who broke new paths into the once unknown. As early as

1859, Mr. Farmer lighted his whole house with electric lights, and blew up a little ship by a tiny submarine torpedo in 1847, and in the same year propelled by electricity a car carrying passengers. Yet neither of these names is found in the majority of ordinary cyclopedias or books of reference.

Familiar with such facts, both by a general observation of life, and by a special and critical study of the literature of patents and inventions, Carleton felt perfectly willing to devote himself to a work that he knew would yield but little popular applause, even when victory should be won, — the abolition of railway level or " grade " crossings.

During a brief morning call on Carleton, shortly after he had been elected Senator in the Massachusetts Legislature for the session of 1890, I asked him what he proposed especially to do. " Well," said he, " I think that if I can get all grade crossings abolished from the railroads of the whole Commonwealth, it will be a good winter's work."

Forthwith he set himself to study the problem, to master resources and statistics, to learn the relation between capital invested and profits made by the railway corporation, and especially to measure the forces in favor of and in opposition to the proposed reform.

About this time, the chief servant of Shawmut Church was studying an allied question. While the " grade crossing " slew its thousands of non-travelling citizens, the freight-car, with its link-and-pin coupling, its block-bumpers, its hand-brakes, its slippery roofs, its manifold shiftings over frogs and switches, slew its tens of thousands of railway operatives. On the grade crossings, the victims were chiefly old, deaf, or blind men and women, cripples, children, drunkards, and miscellaneous people. On the other hand, the freight-cars killed almost exclusively the flower of the country's manhood. The tens of thousands of hands crushed between bumpers, of arms and legs cut off, of bodies broken and mangled, were, in the majority of cases, those of healthy, intelligent men, between the ages of eighteen and fifty, and usually breadwinners for whole families. The slaughter every year was equal to that of a battle at Waterloo or Gettysburg. Fairy tales about monsters devouring human beings, legends of colossal dragons swallowing annually

their quota of fair virgins, were insignificant
expressions of damage done to the human race
compared to that annual tribute poured into
the insatiable maw of the railway Moloch.
Every great line of traffic, like the Pennsylvania or New York Central Railway, ate up a
man a day. Sometimes, between sunrise and
sunset, a single road made four or five widows,
with a profusion of orphans.

Yet two men, each of the name of Coffin,
and each of that superb Nantucket stock
which has enriched our nation and carried the
American flag to every sea, were working in
the West and the East, for the abolition of
legalized slaughter. Lorenzo Coffin, of Iowa,
a distant cousin of Carleton's, whom so many
railway men always salute as " father," had
been for years trying to throttle the two twin
enemies of the railway man, alcohol, and the
freight-car equipment of link-and-pin coupler
and hand-brake. It was he who agitated un-
ceasingly for national protection to railway
men, and to the brakeman especially. He
and his fellow reformers asked for a law compelling the use of a brake which would relieve
the crew from such awful exposure and fool-

hardy risk of life on the icy roofs of the cars in winter, and for couplers which, by abolishing the iron link and pin, would save the constant and almost certain crushing of the hands which the shifting of the cars compelled when coupled in the old way.

For a long time Lorenzo Coffin's efforts seemed utterly useless. This was simply because human life was cheaper than machinery, and because public opinion on this particular subject had not yet become Christian. It was Jesus Christ who raised the value of both the human body and the human soul, abolished gladiatorial shows, raised up hospitals, created cemeteries, even for the poorest, made life insurance companies possible, and put even such value on human life as could be recovered in action by law from corporations which murder men through sordid economy or criminal carelessness. Lorenzo Coffin wrought for the application of Christianity to railway men. When finally the law was passed, compelling safety-couplers and air-brakes, and when, in the constitution of New York State, the limit of five thousand dollars replevin for a human life destroyed by a corporation was abolished, and no limit set, there were two new triumphs of Christianity. In these phenomena, we see only further illustrations of that Kingdom of Heaven proclaimed by Christ, and illustrated both in the hidden leaven and the phenomenal mustard-seed.

A sermon by the pastor of Shawmut Church, on " Lions that devour," depicted the great American slaughter-field. It set forth the array of figures as given him in the reports of the Inter-State Commerce Commission, sent by his friend, the Hon. Augustus Schoonmaker, of Kingston, New York, and then in Washington, one of the Commissioners. There was considerable surprise and criticism from among his auditors, and the facts as set forth were doubted. There were present, as usual on Sunday mornings in Shawmut Church, men of public affairs, presidents of banks, the collector of the port of Boston, a general in the regular army, a veteran colonel of volunteers, several officers of railway companies, and, most of all, Mr. Charles Carleton Coffin. He and they thought the statements given of the slaughter of young men on railroads in the United States must be incredible. Even Carleton had not then informed himself concerning that great field of blood extending from ocean to ocean, and from the Great Lakes to the Gulf, which every year was strewn with the corpses or mangled limbs of twenty-five thousand people. He thought his friend in the pulpit must be mistaken, and frankly told him so.

On the following Sunday, having received the figures for the current year, from the best authority in Washington, the preacher was able to say that his statements of last Sunday had been below reality, and that, instead of exaggerating, he had underestimated the facts. This gave Mr. Coffin, as he afterwards confessed, fresh impetus in his determination to get grade crossings abolished in Massachusetts.

Having first personally interviewed the presidents of several great railroads leading out from Boston, and finding one or two heartily in favor of the idea, two or three more not in opposition, and scarcely a majority opposed, he persevered. He pressed the matter, and the bill was carried and signed by the governor. It provided that within a term of years all grade crossings in Massachusetts should be abolished. This will require the expenditure of many millions of dollars, the sinking or elevating of tracks, and the making of tunnels and bridges. The work was nobly begun. At this moment, in May, 1898, the progress is steadily forward to the great consummation.

Though his measure for the protection of human life received very little popular notice, Carleton counted it one of the best things that God had allowed him to do. And certainly, among the noble and truly Christian measures for the good of society, in this last decade of the century, the work done by Lorenzo Coffin in Iowa, as well as in the country at large, and by Senator Charles Carleton Coffin in Massachusetts, — a State whose example will be followed by others, — must ever be remembered by the grateful student of social progress. Surely, Carleton proved himself not merely a politician, but a statesman.

The welfare of the city of Boston was ever dear to Carleton's heart. He gave a great deal of time and thought to thinking out problems affecting its welfare, and hence was often a welcome speaker at club meetings, which are so numerous, so delightful, and, certainly, in their number, peculiar to Boston. He wrote for the press, giving his views freely, whenever any vital question was before the people. This often entailed severe labor and the sacrifice of time to one who could never boast very much of this world's goods.

When the writer first, in 1886, came to Boston to live, he found the horse everywhere in the city; when he left it in 1893 there was only the trolley. The motor power was carried through the air from a central source. It is even yet, however, a test of one's knowledge of Boston — a city not laid out by William Penn, but by cows and admirers of crookedness — to understand the street-car system of the city. Most of the street passenger lines fell gradually into the hands of one great corporation, which vastly improved the service, enlarging and making more comfortable, not to say luxurious, the accommodations, and by unification enabling one to ride astonishing distances for a nickel coin.

From the peculiar shape of the city and the converging of the thoroughfares on Tremont Street, fronting the Common and the old burying grounds, the space between Boylston Street and Cornhill was, at certain hours of the day, in a painful state of congestion. Then the stoppage of the cars, the loss of time, and the waste of temper was something which no nineteenth century man could stand with equanimity. How to relieve the congestion was the difficulty. Should there be an elevated railway, or a new avenue opened through the midst of the city? This was the question.

To this subject, Carleton gave his earnest attention. He remembered the day when the now elegant region of the Back Bay was marsh and water, when schooners discharged coal and lumber in that Public Garden, which in June looks like a day of heaven on earth, and when Tremont Street stopped at the crossing of the Boston and Albany railway. Even as late as 1850 the population included within the ten-mile radius of the city hall was but 267,861; in 1890, the increase was to 841,-617; and the same ratio of increase will give, in 1930, 2,700,000 souls. In 1871, seventeen million people were moved into Boston by steam; in 1891, fifty-one millions. At the same ratio of increase, on the opening of the twentieth century, there will be 100,000,000 persons riding in from the suburbs, and of travellers in the street-cars, in A. D. 1910, nearly half a billion.

Carleton, the engineer and statesman, believed that neither a subway nor an elevated railway would solve the problem. He spoke, lectured, and wrote, in favor of a central city viaduct. For both surface and elevated railways, he proposed an avenue eighty feet wide, making a clear road from Tremont to Causeway Streets.

Moreover, he believed that the city should own the roads that should transport passengers within the city limits. He was not afraid of that kind of socialism which provides for the absolute necessities of modern associated life. He expected great amelioration to come to society from the breaking up and passing away of the old relics of feudalism, as well as of the power of the privileged man as against man, of wealth against commonwealth. He believed that transportation within city limits should be under public ownership and control. He therefore opposed the subway and the incorporation of the Boston Elevated Railroad Company.

One of his most vigorous letters, occupying a column and a half, in the Boston *Herald* of July 17, 1895, is a powerful plea for the rejection by the people of an act which should give the traffic of the streets of Boston and surrounding municipalities into the hands of a corporation for all time. He considered that the act, which had been rushed through the legislature in one day at the close of the session, was a hasty piece of patchwork made by dovetailing two bills together, and was highly objectionable. He wrote:

" Why shall the people give away their own rights? Do they not own the ground beneath the surface and the air above the surface? . . . What need is there of a corporation? Cannot the people in their sovereign capacity do for themselves all that a corporation can do? Why give away their rights, and burden themselves with taxes for the benefit of a corporation?

" Does some one say it is a nationalistic idea? Then it is nationalism for Boston to own Quincy Market, the water supply, the system of sewerage. Far different from governmental ownership of railroads, with the complications of interstate commerce, is the

proposition for public ownership of street railways. A street is a highway. Why shall not
the subway under the street, or the structure
over it, be a highway, built and owned by the
people, and for their use and benefit, and not
for the enrichment of a corporation ? "

After forcibly presenting the reasonable objections to the bill, he closed by pleading that
it be rejected, and that the next legislature be
asked to establish a metropolitan district and
the appointment of a commission with full
power to do everything that could be done
under the bill, " not for the greed of a corporation, but for the welfare of the people."

CHAPTER XXVII

CARLETON'S biographer having resigned the pastorate of Shawmut Church at the end of 1892, the work was continued by the Rev. William E. Barton, who had been called from Wellington, Ohio. He began his ministrations March 1, 1893. As so very many families forming the old church, and who had grown up in it from early manhood, youth, or even childhood, had removed from the neighborhood, it was necessary to reorganize to a certain extent. The great changes which had come over the South End, and the drift of population to the more attractive neighborhoods in the Back Bay, Brookline, Dorchester, Newton, Allston, and other beautiful suburbs of Boston, caused much derangement of previously existing conditions. The tremendous development of the means of transportation by the steam, horse or electric railways, to say nothing of the bicycle, had caused a marvellous bloom of new life and flush of vigor among the suburban churches, while those in the older parts of the city suffered corresponding decline. The Shawmut Church, like the Mount Vernon, the Pine Street, and others, had to pass through experiences which make a familiar story to those who know Philadelphia, New York, and London. The work of the old city churches had been to train up and graduate sons and daughters with noble Christian principles and character, to build up the waste places and the newer societies. Like bees, the new swarms out from the old hives were called to gather fresh honey.

The exodus from rural New England and from Canada enlarged Boston, and caused the building up and amazing development of Brookline. With such powerful magnets drawing away the old residents, together with the multiplication of a new and largely non-American and Roman Catholic population into the district lying east of Washington Street, the older congregations of the South End had, by 1890, been vastly changed. Several had been so depleted in their old supporters, that churches moved in a body to new edifices on the streets and avenues lying westward. In others the burdens of support fell upon a decreasing number of faithful men and women. Where once were not enough church edifices to accommodate the people who would worship in them, was now a redundancy. In the city where a Roman Catholic church was once a curiosity are now nearly fifty churches that acknowledge the Pope's supremacy.

These things are stated with some detail, in order to show the character of Charles Carleton Coffin in its true light. After a laborious life, having borne the heat and burden of the day in the churches where his lot was cast, withal, having passed his three score and ten years, one would naturally expect this veteran to seek repose. Not a few of his friends looked to see him set himself down in some one of the luxurious new church edifices, amid congenial social surroundings and material comforts.

Carleton sought not his own comfort. When the new pastor and the old guard, left in Shawmut Church to " hold the fort," took counsel together as to the future, they waited with some anxiety to hear what choice and decision Mr. Coffin would make. He had already selected the ground and was making plans for building his new home, " Alwington," at No. 9 Shailer Street, Brookline, — several miles away from his old residence in Dartmouth Street. It was naturally thought that he would ally himself with a wealthy old church elsewhere, and bid farewell, as so many had done, to their old church home, taking no new burdens, risks, or responsibilities. During the conference in the Shawmut prayer-room, Carleton rose and, with a smiling face and his usual impressive manner, stated that he should give his hopes and prayers, his sympathy and work, his gifts and influence to Shawmut Church; and, for the present at least, without dictating the future, would cast in his lot with the Shawmut people. A thrill of delight, unbidden tears of joy, and a new warmth of heart came to those who heard. As time went on he so adjusted himself to the change, and found Dr. Barton such a stimulating preacher, that any thought of sacrifice entirely vanished.

When the first Congregational Church of

Christ in Ithaca, N. Y.,—the city named by Simeon DeWitt after his Ulysses-like wanderings were over,—sent out its "letter missive" to the churches of the Central Association of New York State, and to Shawmut Church in Boston, the latter responded. It was voted to send, as their messengers, the pastor, Rev. Dr. Barton, and Mr. Coffin; Mrs. Barton and Mrs. Coffin accompanied them. These four came on to the Forest City and its university "far above Cayuga's waters." With the delight of a boy Carleton enjoyed the marvellously lovely scenery, the hills robed in colors as many as though they had borrowed Joseph's robe, and Cayuga, the queen of the waters in New York's beautiful lake region. Most of all he visited with delight that typical American university which, Christian in spirit, neither propagates nor attacks the creed of any sect.

With its stately edifices for culture, training, research, and religion, it had risen like a new city on the farm of Ezra Cornell. This far-seeing man, like Mr. Coffin, had, when so many others were blind, discerned in the new force, electricity, the vast future benefits to commerce, science, and civilization. Ezra Cornell had helped powerfully to develop its application by his thought, his money, and his personal influence. Ezra Cornell, in Irish phrase, "invented telegraph poles." Moses Farmer, the electrician, invented the lineman's spurred irons by which to climb them.

Besides attending the Church Council in the afternoon, Carleton made an address in the evening that was to one flattering and to many inspiring. Later on, the same night, he attended the reception given to the Faculty and new students at the house of President J. G. Schurman. He was delighted in seeing the young president, with whose power as a thinker and writer he had already acquainted himself.

Carleton's last and chief literary work, done in his old home on Dartmouth Street, was to link together in the form of story the Revolutionary lore which he had gathered up from talks with participators in "the time that tried men's souls." From boyhood's memories, from long and wide reading in original monographs, from topographical acquaintance, he planned to write a trio or quartet of stories of American history. He wished to present the scenes of the Revolution as in the bright colors of reality, in the dark shadows which should recall sacrifice, and with that graphic detail and power to turn the past into the present, of which he was a master.

As he had repeatedly written the story of the great Civil War from the point of view of a war correspondent actually on the ground, so would he tell the story of the Revolution as if he had been a living and breathing witness of what went on from day to day, enjoying and suffering those hopes and fears which delight and torment the soul when the veil of the future still hangs opaque before the mind.

His first instalment, "The Daughters of the Revolution," was published by Messrs. Houghton, Mifflin & Co., in a comely and well-illustrated volume. It deals with that opening history of the eight years' war with Great Britain which at the beginning had Boston for its centre and in which New England especially took part.

In his other books, "Building the Nation," "Boys of '76," and "Old Times in the Colonies," Carleton had not ignored the work and influence of the "home guard" composed of mothers, daughters, aunts, cousins, and grandmothers; but in this story of the "Daughters" he gave special prominence to what our female ancestors did to make the country free, and to hand down in safeguarded forms that which had been outraged by King and Parliament.

How widely popular this volume may have been, the writer cannot say, but he knows that one little maiden whom he sees every day has re-read the work several times.

In a subsequent volume of the series, Carleton proposed to repicture the splendid achievements of the colonial army in northeastern New York. Here, from Lake Champlain to Sandy Hook, is a "great rift valley" which lies upon the earth's scarred and diversified surface like a mighty trough. It corresponds to that larger and grander rift valley from Lebanon to Zanzibar, through Galilee and the Jordan, the Red Sea, and the great Nyanzas, or Lakes of Africa. As in the oldest gash on the earth's face lies the scene of a long procession of events, so, of all places on the American continent, probably, no line of territory has witnessed such a succession of dramatic, brilliant, and decisive events, both in unrecorded time and in historic days, from Champlain and Henry Hudson to the era of Fulton, Morse, and Edison.

In the Revolution, the Green Mountain boys, and the New York and New England militia under Schuyler and Gates, had made this region the scene of one of the decisive campaigns of the world. Yet, in the background and at home, the heroines did their noble part in working for that consummation at Saratoga which won the recognition and material aid of France for the United States of America. Besides Lafayette, came also the lilies of France, alongside the stars and stripes. The white uniforms were set in battle array with the buff and blue against the red coats, and herein Carleton saw visions and dreamed dreams, which his pen, like the camera which chains the light, was to photograph in words. He had made his preliminary studies, readings, personal interviews, and reëxamination of the region, and had written four or five chapters, when the call of the Captain to another detail of service came to him.

Life is worth living as long as one is interested in other lives than one's own. " *Dando conservat*" is the motto of a famous Dutch-American family. So Carleton, by giving, preserved. In the summer of 1895, after Japan had startled the world by her military prowess, Carleton went down to Nantucket Island, and there at a great celebration delivered a fine historical address, closing with these words:

" Thus it came to pass that he who guides the sparrow in its flight saw fit to use the sailors of Nantucket, by shipwreck and imprisonment, as his agents to bring about the resurrection of the millions of Japan from the grave of a dead past to a new and vigorous life. Thus it is that Nantucket occupies an exalted position in connection with the history of our country."

Of this he wrote me in one of his last letters, February 27, 1896:

" I have read ' Townsend Harris ' with unspeakable delight. I love to think of the resurrection of Japan in connection with the Puritans of Massachusetts,—the original movement culminating in Perry's expedition having its origin in the shipwrecking of Nantucket sailors on the shores of that empire." Mr.

Coffin brought out this idea in his earlier and later address which he gave at Nantucket.

Having lived over thirteen years, from 1877 to 1895, at No. 81 Dartmouth Street, and feeling now the need for a little more quiet from the rumble of the trolley-car, for more light and room, for house space, for the accommodation of friends who loved to make their home with a genial host and his loving companion, and to indulge in that hospitality which was a lifelong trait, Mr. and Mrs. Coffin began looking for a site whereon to build in Brookline. No yokefellows were ever more truly one in spirit than "Uncle Charles and Aunt Sally." Providence having denied them the children for whom they had yearned, both delighted in a constant stream of young people and friends. Blessed by divine liberality in the form of nephews and nieces, rich in the gifts of nature, culture, and grace, neither Carleton nor his wife was often left lonely.

The new house was built after his suggestions and under his own personal oversight, the outdoor tasks and journeys thus necessitated making a variety rather pleasant than otherwise. Here, in this new home, his golden wedding was to be celebrated, February 18, 1896. The house was in modern style, with all the comforts and conveniences which science and applied art could suggest. While comparatively modest and simple in general plan and equipment, it had open fireplaces, electric lights, a spacious porch, roomy hallways, and plenty of windows. It was No. 9 Shailer Street, and named Alwington, after the ancestral home in Devonshire, England.

Mr. Coffin's study room was upon the northeast, where, with plenty of light and the morning sun, he could sit at his desk looking out upon Harvard Street, and over towards Beacon Street; the opposite side of the street, fortunately, not being occupied by buildings to obscure his view. At first he was often allured from his work for many minutes, and even for a half hour at a time, by a majestic elm-tree so rich in foliage and comely in form that he looked upon it with ravished eyes. It was in this room that he wrote the chapters for his second book, which was to show especially the part which American women had played in the making of their country.

CHAPTER XXVIII

THE HOME AT ALWINGTON

IT was a remarkable coincidence that Mr.
Coffin was to exchange worlds and transfer
his work in the very year in which the issues
of the Civil War were to be eliminated from
national politics, when not one of the several
party platforms was to make any allusion to
the struggle of 1861–65, or to any of its
numerous legacies. In this year, 1896, also,
for the first time since 1860, Southern men, the
one a Confederate general, and the other a
Populist editor, were to be nominated for possible chief magistracy. Mr. Coffin, with prescience, had already seen that the war issues,
grand as they were, had melted away into even
vaster national questions. He had turned his
thoughts towards the solution of problems
which concerned the nation as a whole and
humanity as a race. His historical addresses
and lectures went back to older subjects, while

his thoughts soared forward to the newer conditions, theories, and problems which were
looming in the slowly unveiling future.　In
literature he turned, and gladly, too, from the
scenes of slavery and war between brothers.
With his pen he sought to picture the ancient
heroisms, in the story of which the people of the
States of rice and cotton, as well as of granite,
ice, and grain, were alike interested, as in a
common heritage.　In Alwington, surrounded
by old and new friends, genial and cultured,
he hoped, if it were God's will, to complete his
work with a rotunda-like series of pen pictures
of the Revolution.

This was not to be, though he was to die
"in harness," like Nicanor of old, without lin-
gering illness or broken powers.　While he
was to see not a few golden days of A. D. 1896,
yet the proposed pictures were to be left upon
the easel, scarcely more than begun.　The
pen and ink on his table were to remain, like
brushes on the palette, with none to finish as
the master-workman had planned.

Months before that date of February 18th,
on which their golden wedding was to be celebrated, Mr. and Mrs. Coffin had secured my

promise that I should be present. Coming on to Boston, I led the morning worship in the Eliot Church of Newton, which is named after the apostle of the Indians, the quarter-millennial anniversary of the beginning of whose work at Nonantum has just been celebrated. In the afternoon, I had the pleasure of looking into the faces of three score or more of my former Shawmut parishioners in the Casino hall in Beaconsfield Terrace.

Mr. Coffin had, from the first, fully agreed with the writer in believing that a Congregational church should be formed in the Reservoir district, which had, he predicted, a brilliant and substantial future. He was among the very first to move for the sale of the old property on Tremont Street, and he personally prepared the petition to the Legislature of Massachusetts for permission to sell and move. Afterwards, when the new enterprise seemed to have been abandoned, he listened to the call of duty and remained in Shawmut Church. When he became a resident in Brookline, feeling it still his duty to work and toil, to break new paths, to make the road straight for his Master, rather than to sit down at ease in

Zion, he cast his lot in with a little company of those who, though few and without wealth, bravely and hopefully resolved to form a church where it was needed. On November 3d, they first gathered for worship, and one year later, November 4, 1896, the church was formed, with Rev. Harris G. Hale as pastor, and taking the historic, appropriate, but uncommon name, Leyden. Their first collection of money, as a thank-offering to God, was for Foreign Missions.

On that afternoon of February 16th, Carleton was present, joining heartily in the worship. As usual, he listened with that wonderfully luminous face of his and that close attention to the discourse, which, like the cable-ships, ran out unseen telegraphy of sympathy. The service, and the usual warm grasping of hands and those pleasant social exchanges for which the Shawmut people were so noted, being over, some fifteen or twenty gathered in the hospitable library of M. F. Dickinson, Jr., whose home was but a few rods off, on the other side of Beacon Street. After a half hour of sparkling reminiscences of the dear old days in Shawmut, all had gone except the host, Mr.

Coffin, and the biographer, who then had not even a passing thought of the work he was soon to do. As Carleton sat there in an easy chair before the wood-fire on the open hearth, his feet stretched out comfortably upon the tiles, and his two hands, with their finger and thumb tips together, as was his usual custom when good thinking and pleasant conversation went on together, he talked about the future of Boston and of Congregational Christianity.

Interested as I was, a sudden feeling of pain seized me as I noticed how sunken were his eyes. I am not a physician, but I have seen many people die. I have looked upon many more as they approached their mortal end, marked with signs which they saw not, nor often even their friends observed, but which were as plain and readable as the stencilled directions upon freight to be sent and delivered elsewhere. After a handshake and an invitation from him to dine the next night at his house, and to be at the golden wedding on Tuesday, we bade him good afternoon. On returning with my host in front of the fire, I said, "I feel sad, for our friend Mr.

Coffin is marked for early death; he will certainly not outlive this year."

Nevertheless, I could not but count Charles Carleton Coffin among the number of those whom God made rich in the threefold life of body, soul, and spirit.

The old Greeks, whose wonderfully rich experience of life, penetrating insight, powers of analysis, and gift of literary expression enabled them to coin the words to fitly represent their thoughts, knew how to describe both love and life better than we, having a mintage of thought for each in its threefold form. As they discriminated *eros*, *philé*, and *agapé* in love, so also they put difference between *psyché*, *bios*, and *zoé* in life.

What other ranges of existence and developments of being there may be for God's chosen ones in worlds to come, we dare not conjecture, but this we know. Carleton had even then, as I saw him marked for an early change of worlds, entered into threefold life.

1. The lusty boy and youth, the mature man with not a perfect, yet a sound, physical organization, showed a good specimen of the human animal, rich in the breath of life, —*psyché*.

2. The long and varied career of farmer, surveyor, citizen, Christian interested in his fellows and their welfare, with varied work, travel, and adventure, manifested the noble *bios*, — the career or course of strenuous endeavor.

3. The spiritual attainments in character, the ever outflowing benevolence, the kindly thought, the healing sunshine of his presence, the calm faith, the firm trust in God, gave assurance of the *zoé*.

These three stages of existence revealed Carleton as one affluent with what men call life, and of which the young ever crave more, and also in that "life which is life indeed," which survives death, which is the extinction of the *psyché* or animal breath, — the soul remaining as the abode of the spirit. In body, soul, and spirit, Charles Carleton Coffin was a true man, who, even in the evening of life, was rich in those three forms of life which God has revealed and discriminated through the illuminating Greek language of the New Testament.

True indeed it was that, while with multiplying years the animal life lessened in quantity and intensity, the spiritual life was enriched and deepened ; or, to put it in Paul's language and in the historical present so favored by Carleton, " While the outward man perisheth, the inward man is renewed day by day."

CHAPTER XXIX

THE GOLDEN WEDDING

THUS, amid happy surroundings, in the new home, in the last leap-year of this wonderful century, came the time of the golden wedding. God had walked with these, his children, fifty years, while they had walked with one another. Providence seemed to whisper, " Come, for all things are now ready." The new home was finished and furnished, all bright and cheerful, and suffused with the atmosphere of genial companionship. The bride of a half century before, now with the roses of health blooming under the trellis of her silvery hair, with sparkling eyes beaming fun and sympathy, welcome and gladness, by turns, was at this season in happy health. This was largely owing, as she gladly acknowledged, to regular calisthenics, plenty of fresh air, and complete occupation of mind and body. The thousand invitations in gilt and white had,

as with " the wings of a dove covered with silver and her feathers with yellow gold," flown
over the city, commonwealth, and nation.   On
February 18th, the house having been transformed by young friends into a maze of
greenery and flowers, husband and wife stood
together to receive congratulations.   In the
hall were ropes of sturdy pine boughs and
glistening laurel, with a huge wreath of ever-
green suspended from the ceiling, and bearing
the anniversary date, 1846 and 1896.   In the
reception-room one friend had hung the em-
blem of two hearts joined by a band of gold
above the cornice.   Dining-room and library
were festooned with smilax.   In the archways
and windows were hanging baskets of jonquils
and ferns.   "An help meet for him," the bride
of fifty years was arrayed in heliotrope satin
with trimmings of point lace, making, as we
thought, with her delicate complexion and soft
white hair, a sight as lovely as when, amid the
snow-storms of New Hampshire, a half century
before, Charles Carleton Coffin first called Sallie
Farmer his wife.

Of Washington it has been said, " God
made him childless that a nation might call

him father."   In the home on that day were
scores of nieces and nephews, and children of
several generations, from the babe in arms, and
the child with pinafore, to the stately dames
and long-bearded men, who, one and all, called
the bride and groom " uncle and aunt." From
a ladies' orchestra, on the top floor, music filled
the house, the melody falling like a lark's song
in upper air.   In the dining-room, turned for
the nonce into a booth of evergreens, where
everything was sparkle and joy, new and old
friends met to discuss, over dainty cups and
plates, both the happy moment and the de-
lights of long ago.

It was not only a very bright, but a note-
worthy company that gathered on that February afternoon and evening. Massachusetts was
about to lose by death her Governor, F. T.
Greenhalge, as she had lost three ex-Gover-
nors, all friends of Carleton, within the previous twelvemonth, but there was present the
handsome acting-Governor of the Commonwealth, Roger Wolcott.   Men eminent in
political life, authors, editors, preachers, business men, troops of lifelong friends, men and
women of eminence, honor, and usefulness,

fellow Christians and workers in wonderfully varied lines of activity, were present to share in and add to the joy. Among the gifts, which seemed to come like Jupiter's shower of gold upon Danaë, were two that touched Carleton very deeply. The Massachusetts Club, which has numbered in its body many Senators, Governors, generals, diplomatists, lawyers, authors, and merchants, whose names shine very high on the roll of national fame, sent their fellow member an appropriate present. Instead of the regular cup, vase, or urn, or anything that might suggest stress, strain, or even victory, or even minister to personal vanity, the Club, through its secretary, Mr. S. S. Blanchard, presented the master of Alwington with a superb steel engraving, richly framed. It represented the Master, sitting under the vine-roof trellis at the home of Lazarus, in Bethlehem. "You knew just what I wanted," whispered the happy receiver.

During the evening, when the people of Shawmut Church were present, a hundred or more strong, their former and latter chief servant being with them, a silver casket, with twenty half eagles in it, was presented by Dr.

W. E. Barton, with choice and fitting words. So deeply affected was this man Carleton, so noted for his self-mastery, that, for a moment, those who knew him best were shot through as by a shaft of foreboding, lest, then and there, the horses and chariot of fire might come for the prophet. A quarter of a minute's pause, understood by most present as nothing more than a natural interval between presentation speech and reply, and then Carleton, as fully as his emotion would admit, uttered fitting words of response.

The " banquet hall deserted," the photographic camera was brought into requisition, and pleasant souvenirs of a grand occasion were made. Everything joyously planned had been happily carried out. This was the culminating event in the life of a good man, to the making of whom, race, ancestry, parentage, wife, home, friends, country, and opportunity had contributed, and to all of which and whom, under God, Carleton often made grateful acknowledgments.

It was but a fortnight after this event, in which I participated with such unalloyed pleasure, that the telegraphic yellow paper, with its type-script message, announced that the earthly house of the tabernacle of Carleton's spirit had been dissolved, and that his building of God, the " house not made with hands," had been entered.

The story of Carleton's last thirteen days on earth is soon told. He had written a little upon his new story. For the *Boston Journal* he had penned an article calling attention to the multiplying " sky-scraper " houses, and the need of better fire-apparatus. He had, with the physician's sanction, agreed to address on Monday evening, March 2d, the T. Starr King Unitarian Club of South Boston, on " Some Recollections of a War Correspondent."

Carleton's last Sunday on earth was as one of " the days of heaven upon earth." It was rich to overflowing with joyous experiences. It is now ours to see that the shadows of his sunset of life were pointing to the eternal morning.

It was the opening day of spring. At Shawmut Church, in holy communion, he, with others, celebrated the love of his Saviour and Friend. To Carleton, it was a true Eucharist. A new vision of the cross and its meaning seemed to dawn upon his soul. At the supper - table, conversation turned upon Christ's obedience unto death, his great reconciliation of man to God, his power to move men, the crucifixion, and its meaning. Carleton said, after expressing his deep satisfaction with Doctor Barton's morning sermon, and his interpretation of the atonement, that he regarded Christ's life as the highest exhibition of service. By his willing death on the cross, Jesus showed himself the greatest and best of all servants of man, while thus joyfully doing his Father's will. On that day of rest, Carleton seemed to dwell in an almost transfigurating atmosphere of delight in his Master.

On Sunday night husband and wife enjoyed a quiet hour, hand in hand, before the wood fire. The sunlight and warmth of years gone by, coined into stick and fagots from the forest, were released again in glow and warmth, making playful lights and warning shadows. The golden minutes passed by. The prattle of lovers and the sober wisdom of experience blended. Then, night's oblivion. Again, the cheerful morning meal and the merry company, the incense of worship, and the separation of each and all to the day's toil.

Carleton sat down in his study room to write. He soon called his wife, complaining of a distressing pain in his stomach. He was advised to go to bed, and did so. The physician, Dr. A. L. Kennedy, was sent for. "How is your head?" asked Doctor Kennedy.

"If it were not for this pain, I should get up and write," answered Carleton.

With the consent of the physician he rose from the couch and walked the room for awhile for relief. Then returning, as he was about to lie down again, he fell over. Quickly unconscious, he passed away. Science would call the immediate cause of death apoplexy.

Thus died at his post, as he would have wished, the great war correspondent, traveller, author, statesman, and friend of man and God. He had lived nearly three years beyond the allotted period of three score and ten.

Two days later, while the flag over the public schoolhouse in Brookline drooped at half-mast, and Carleton's picture was wreathed with laurels, at the request of the scholars themselves, in the impressive auditorium of Shaw-

mut Church, Carleton's body lay amid palms
and lilies in the space fronting the pulpit. At
his head and at his feet stood a veteran-senti-
nel from the John A. Andrew Post of the
Grand Army of the Republic. These were
relieved every quarter of an hour, during the
exercises, by comrades who had been detailed
for a service which they were proud to render
to one who had so well told their story and
honored them so highly. It was entirely a
voluntary offering on the part of the veterans
to pay this tribute of regard, which was as
touching as it was unostentatious.

Nowhere in the church edifice were there any
of the usual insignia of woe. The dirge was
at first played to express the universal grief in
the music of the organ, but it soon melted into
In Memoriam and hymns of triumph. The
quartet sang "Jesus Reigns," a favorite
hymn of Carleton's, to music which he had
himself composed only two years before.

It reminded me of the burst of melody
which, from the belfry of the church in a
Moravian town, announces the soul's farewell
to earth and birth into heaven.

In the audience which filled the pews downstairs were men and women eminent in every walk of life, representatives of clubs, societies, and organizations. Probably without a single exception, all were sincere mourners, while yet rejoicing in a life so nobly rounded out. In the pulpit sat two of the pastors of Shawmut Church, and Dr. Arthur Little, friend of Carleton's boyhood, and a near relative. The eulogies were discriminating.

The addresses, with the prayers offered and the tributes made in script or print, with some letters of condolence received by Mrs. Coffin, and a remarkable interesting biographical sketch from *The Congregationalist*, by Rev. Howard A. Bridgman, have been gathered in a pamphlet published by George H. Wright, Harcourt Street, Boston.

From this pamphlet we extract the following :

After prayer and a brief silence, Dr. Little said :

" There are few men, I think, engrossed in the affairs of life, for an entire generation, to whom the Word of God was so vital and so precious as to our friend, Mr. Coffin. Let us open this Word, and listen while God speaks to us, in Ps. 23 ; Ps. 39 : 4, 13 ; Ps. 46 : 1, 5, 7.

"I will read from Ezekiel 26 : 1–5, which was a favorite word with Mr. Coffin, and the passage which he himself read, as he was journeying in the Eastern land, at the very spot concerning which the prophecy is uttered. Mr. Coffin was sitting there with his open Bible, and saw the literal fulfilment of this prophecy, — the fishermen spreading the nets in the very neighborhood where he was sitting."

The continued readings were from John 11 : 21, 23; John 14 : 19; 2 Cor. 5 : 1, 8; Rev. 21 : 1; Rev. 22 : 5; 1 Cor. 15 : 51, 57. The quartet sang "In My Father's Arms Enfolded."

Dr. Barton then read a letter from Rev. E. B. Webb, D. D., who was unable to be present. The following are the closing paragraphs. They recall the Oriental travels enjoyed by pastor and parishioner in company.

"Together we visited the home of Mary and Martha, and the tomb from which the Life-Giver called forth Lazarus to a new and divine life. We stood in Gethsemane, by the old olive-trees, beneath the shadows of which the Saviour of men prayed, and sweat, as it were, great drops of blood. We climbed together to the top of the Mount of Olives, and looked up into the deep heavens to which he ascended, and abroad to the city over which he wept; and both our words and our silence told how real it all was, and how the significance of it entered into our lives.

"From the city we journeyed northward,—up past Bethel, where Jacob saw a new vision, and got a new heart, and on, past the blue waters of Galilee, and across the great plain, — battle-ground of the ancient nations, — and over the Lebanons to Damascus and Baalbec, and then to the sea, and homeward thence; and always and everywhere scrutinizing the present, or reaching back into the past; drinking from the sparkling waters of Abana and Pharpar, or searching for the wall over which Paul was let down in a basket; impressed by the ruins of half-buried temples and cities, or looking forward, with sublime faith in the prophecy and promise, to the time when all things shall be made new; — Carleton was always the same thoughtful, genial, courteous companion and sympathizing friend.

"I honored, loved, and esteemed the man. His life is a beautiful example of devout Christian steadfastness. The history of his small beginnings, gradual increase, and final success, is one to inspire noble endeavor, and ensure reward. He honored the church, and the church does well to honor him.

"Affectionately yours,

"E. B. WEBB."

The Rev. Dr. Little paid a warm tribute to the memory of his friend:

"At eleven years of age he [Carleton] entered the church. Think of it! Sixty-three years devoted to the service of his Lord and Master! He seems to me to be an illustration of a man who, when he is equal to it, finds a hard physical environment united with a wholesome moral and spiritual environment of supreme advantage. To a weak nature it would very likely mean only failure, but to a man of the heroic mould of Mr. Coffin it meant opportunity, and it only nerved him to more strenuous effort; and it was everything to him that the atmosphere in the home, the community, and the church was what it was, — so warm, so Christian, so spiritual, so sympathetic, and so suited to furnish just the right conditions for the moulding of his very responsive and susceptible nature.

"And then he possessed what I think might very well be called the spirit of aggressiveness, or, possibly better, the spirit of sanctified self-assertion. He never thought of self-assertion for his own sake, or for the sake of honor or promotion, but he had in him a kind of push and an earnestness of purpose — you might almost say audacity — that somehow stirred him and prompted him always to be in the place of greatest advantage at a given time for the service of others. He seemed always to be just at the point of supreme advantage in a crisis, just where he could give the world, at the right time, and in the best way, the fullest report of a battle, or a conference, or any other matters of supreme moment. This was characteristic of him.   It appeared all through his New Hampshire life, and was indeed in part a native endowment."

After an address by the author of this volume on "Charles Carleton Coffin as a Historian," Dr. W. E. Barton, in felicitous diction, reviewed the earthly life of him with whose career many memories were then busy.

"Grief is no unusual thing.   There is no heart here that has not known it.   There is scarce a home where death has not entered.   We weep the more sincerely with those that weep, because the intervals are not long between our own sorrows.   The whole Commonwealth mourns to-day our chief magistrate. God comfort his family!   God save the Commonwealth of Massachusetts!   God bless him in whose elevation to the Governor's chair Providence has anticipated the will of the people.

"A very tender sorrow brings us here to-day, and we turn for comfort to the Word of God.

"Text: With long life will I satisfy him, |and shew him my salvation. — Ps. 91 : 16.

"It is not because of his unusual age that this text seems to me appropriate for the funeral of our friend.   His years were but little more than threescore and ten, and his step was light, and his heart was young, and we hardly thought of him as an old man.   Nor is it because his work seemed to us completed, that we think of the measure of his days as satisfied. His facile pen dropped upon a new page; and before him, as he ceased to labor, were tasks midway, and others just begun. It is because our first feeling is so unsatisfied, it is because there was so much more which he wished, and we wished him to do, and that we are constrained to measure the length of his life, and to find, if we may find, in spite of this sudden break in our hopes and his plans, a completion that can satisfy. Measured by its experiences and accomplishments, it may seem to us that this life, so abruptly terminated, was one whose length and symmetry well deserve to be considered a fulfilment of the promise of the text."

Following the prayer, Dr. Barton said:

"It was the purpose of our organist, Mr. Dunham, a true and honored friend of Mr. Coffin, to play, as the postlude to this service, the stateliest of funeral marches, but I dissuaded him. This is a Christian funeral. Our music is not a dirge, but a jubilate. The hope of our friend in life is ours for him in death. Instead of even the noblest funeral march expressing our own grief, there will be played the most triumphant of anthems, expressing his own victory over death, — Handel's matchless 'Hallelujah Chorus.'"

The organ then played the "Hallelujah Chorus," and the benediction was pronounced by Dr. Barton.

It had been intended to deposit the mortal relics of Carleton in the ancestral cemetery at Webster, N. H., the village next to Boscawen, but Providence interposed. After all preparations for travel and transportation had been made, heavy rains fell, which washed away bridges and so disturbed the ordinary condition of the roads in New Hampshire that the body had to be deposited in a vault at Brookline until a more convenient season for interment. Meanwhile, the soldiers of the Grand Army, adult friends, and even children, united in the wish that the grave of their friend and helper might be within easy reach of Boston, so that on the National Memorial Day, and at other times of visitation, the grassy mound might be accessible for the tribute of flowers. And so it eventuated that what was once mortal of Charles Carleton Coffin rests in Mount Auburn.

The memorial in stone will be a boulder transported from more northern regions ages ago and left by ice on land which belonged to Mrs. Coffin's grandfather. On this rugged New Hampshire granite will be inscribed the name of Charles Carleton Coffin, with the dates of his births into this world and the next.

Both of the man and this, his last memorial, we may say *Deus fecit*.

THE END.